Rescuing Tiffany

Stone Knight's MC
Book 4

Megan Fall

Rescuing Tiffany
Published by Megan Fall

Dedication

To my husband
Craig
Who always has my back!

Contents

Chapter One
Shadow

The wedding had been beautiful. No matter what the brothers said, to rile Trike up, the smile never left his face. He was an extremely happy biker. And, Misty had been a stunning bride. Her white sundress had fit her perfectly, and she wore the prettiest blush all night, as the brothers teased her.

Shadow was happy for the couple. Misty had been through hell. Her brothers girlfriend had tried to kill her, on two separate occasions. The first, was when Misty was still blind, and the girlfriend moved the furniture, so the poor girl fell into a glass coffee table.

And the second time, was when she shot her and blew up a mine, trapping her inside.

Both times Trike had saved her, and now that the threat was eliminated, they could enjoy their time together. Shadow was glad Misty joined the club, because with her came her brother, Noah. Noah had quickly become the brother he was closest to. Both had served in the military, and both were around the same age. Of all the brothers here, he trusted Noah the most.

The last year had been hard on him. He had joined the navy fresh out of high school, and he had loved it. He trained hard and quickly passed the Navy Seal requirements. From there, they had drafted him into a secret branch of the seals. He was known as a Shadow Warrior, and his team could slip in and out of places, undetected.

After five years of that, he was done. He loved his job, and he loved his seal brothers, but the time had come to move on. He knew it was only a matter of time before he was killed in the line of duty. Unfortunately, he had watched many seals die over the years, and he didn't plan to be one of them.

So, for the last year, he had packed a bag, hopped on his Harley, and ridden all over the country. He loved the freedom of the open road, and he loved having no one to answer to even more. But after a while, he decided it was time to find somewhere new to belong. He missed his seal brothers, and he missed the family type relationship they provided.

Three months later, he stopped at a bar, and met Preacher. The man was a bit older than him, but they got along like long lost best friends. Shadow was amazed by the instant friendship that started that day. When he found out Preacher was the president of The Stone Knight's MC, he decided to check it out.

That evening, he became a prospect, and found himself engulfed in a new family. Six months later, he was a fully patched in member. Apparently, most prospects were patched in after a year, but Shadow had proven himself. Plus, with his military background, the brothers decided to cut the probation period in half. And Shadow couldn't be happier.

The wedding was long over now, and there were only about half the brothers wandering around, when Preacher's cell rang. The brothers all stopped talking, to glance his way.

"Preacher," the president growled into the phone. "I'm at a wedding, what the hell do you want?" Then there was silence as the man waited for whoever was on the other end to speak again.

"What," Preacher suddenly bellowed, as he threw his bottle as hard as he could, against the gravel surrounding the fire pit. Then there were rapid fire questions as the brothers looked on in concern.

How long, which direction, and how many men, were growled from Preacher. Then he turned off his phone and roared up at the sky. The brothers stared at Preacher in shock. The man was always calm and controlled, so this meant something was seriously wrong.

"My baby sisters been kidnapped," he finally shared. "I'm leaving in the next fifteen minutes, to rip out the throats of everyone that took her. Anybody that wants can go with me, if they can keep up," he sneered, as he turned and headed for the clubhouse.

The brothers looked at each other in shock, then tore off after their president. Shadow had no idea, that his next decision, was going to completely change his life.

Chapter Two
Shadow

Shadow ran after Preacher, with his brother's right behind him. He was extremely worried about his prez and had no idea what kind of state of mind the man was in.

"Stop," he roared at Preachers back, but the man ignored him and continued on. Finally, Shadow got close enough to grab his arm and spin him around. Preacher caught him with a fist to the chin, but Shadow held his ground.

"Just wait one fucking minute," he growled at the prez. "If this was one of us, you'd be calling church, and telling us to calm the fuck down. So take a fucking minute, sit down, and let us help," he ordered.

Preacher stared at him a minute, then his shoulders drooped, his head dropped, and he whispered brokenly, "I have to get her back."

"I know brother," Shadow said, as he placed his hand on his shoulder. "And, everybody here will help make that happen."

Then, he pushed his prez towards the room they held church in, and made sure he sat down. After yelling at a prospect, and telling to get a whiskey, he made sure Preacher drank it, before they got started. Noah, or Sniper, as he was recently named, was allowed to join them, as his military training would be an asset.

Steele took over the meeting then. "When the fuck did you get a sister," he asked.

Preacher let a half smile grace his lips. "My dad fucked around on my mom when I was eight, hence the baby sister. She lives with her mom, who's a bitch, so I don't get to see her as often as I'd like. She doesn't approve of the biker lifestyle. But regardless, me and Tiffany have stayed close. We see each other as much as we can, and we talk on the phone almost every couple days. She's my baby sister," he finished brokenly.

"Who was on the phone," Dragon asked.

"That was her mother," Preacher told them. "She was the one to call and tell me someone took Tiffany."

"Does she know who took her," Steele questioned.

Preacher looked at Dragon for a minute, then finally said, "The Outlaws."

"Fuck that," Dragon roared. "We killed them all after they took Ali. We put at least a dozen bullets in the president out in the woods," he said as he slammed his first on the table.

"Right," Preacher agreed. "But the president had a brother who has started up a new chapter. He's the one out for blood now, and he took my baby sister. I took out his family, so he's taking out mine."

"So she's dead," Shadow asked in horror.

"Not yet," Preacher said. "Which is why we need to ride now."

"We go in there with guns blazing, they will execute your sister on the spot," Sniper said. "That's always what happens with terrorists. They take out the target, at the first sign of trouble," he explained.

"True," Shadow agreed. "You need one man to go in, friendly like, scope out the place, and get her out. Then he needs to ride like hell and get her here. The war needs to happen on our turf," he said. He turned to Sniper, the only other person with a military background, and silently asked his opinion.

"I completely agree. It's the best way. We could have a few brothers waiting back as protection on the ride back. But the rest of the club could be preparing things here. We have time to arm this place to the nines, and get the girls some place safe," Sniper told them.

Preacher nodded his head, looking a lot more in control now. "That's actually a good idea," he agreed. "But the question is, who goes in after her?"

"I do," Shadow instantly decided. "I'm a trained Shadow Warrior with the Navy Seals. I can go in looking to prospect and get her out that night. I promise no will know until it's too late, that she's gone," he growled. "I'm the best chance you got."

Preached eyed him a minute, then nodded once. After that, all heads were lowered, as the brothers got all the

Intel they could on The Outlaws. But Shadow only had one thing on the brain, saving the poor girl, and bringing her home to her brother. He would make that happen, or he'd sure as hell die trying.

Chapter Three
Shadow

Shadow twisted the throttle and forced his Harley faster down the highway. He had some of his brothers at his back, and they stayed with him, no matter what speed he went. Sniper, his best friend rode beside him, and he appreciated that. He was calmer, knowing the brother was there.

Behind them were, Steele and Dragon, then Navaho and Dagger, and finally Trike and the newest prospect Raid. Apparently, Raid had been Sniper's spotter in the marines, and when Sniper got out, Raid wasn't far behind him. Shadow liked the marine and had a feeling that soon they would be as close as him and Sniper were.

Shadow had fought with Trike, over his decision to come. Trike had only gotten married the previous day, and Shadow wanted him to stay with Misty. Unfortunately, Misty was growing some backbone. She had shoved her finger in Shadow's chest, and growled that when she needed help, the club had been there for her. Now someone else needed help, and she wanted Trike included.

Shadow had been riding for six hours when the cutoff for the exit they discussed in church came up. Trike, Dagger, Steele, Navaho and Raid all saluted him, as they slowed and took the turnoff. He glanced at Sniper, who was the only brother still with him, and he nodded back. Shadow concentrated once again on the road and pushed his bike as fast as it would go.

With the help of Mario, they had discovered that The Outlaws had a clubhouse about eight hours ride away. They decided at the four hour mark, most of the brothers would break off and find some shitty motel to crash in. Shadow and Sniper would ride on for another two hours, then he would break off as well. Shadow would then ride for the last two hours on his own.

On the ride back, he would move fast, and would most likely have Outlaws on his tail. This way he could pick up backup on the way, and the Outlaws wouldn't be expecting it. He was sure trouble would follow him, and the brothers were all armed and ready.

They knew Tiffany had been gone just over four days, but they had no idea what condition she would be in. The Outlaws took her to kill her, but Preacher had heard nothing more, so they were hopeful the girl was still alive. But that didn't mean they hadn't hurt her. When they had gotten Ali back, she was a mess, so Shadow was expecting the worst.

Two hours passed quickly, and soon Sniper was slowing down, and pulling over onto the shoulder. Shadow followed him and stopped behind the brother. Then he powered off his Harley and stepped up to Sniper.

"You ready for this," Sniper asked in concern.

"Ready as I'll ever be," he replied. "If she's alive, I'll get her out," he swore.

"Good enough. You run into trouble, you call, and I'll head to you. I can call the brothers on the way. Don't pull any Lone Ranger shit, play it safe."

"Got it," Shadow agreed. "I'll get in and out, and be back with the girl before you can blink," he said.

Sniper then held out his hand and waited. Shadow shrugged out of his cut, and handed it over, trusting his brother to keep it safe. They had decided that Shadow would ask to prospect, and without his cut, he would look the part. Also, Shadow hadn't been with the club long, so there was a good chance they didn't even know about him.

The brothers embraced and pounded each other on the back. Then Shadow stepped back, as Sniper pulled back out, and took the exit just ahead of them. He watched his brother until he disappeared, then he climbed back on his Harley and started it up. Minutes later he was flying down the highway again, and he had no idea what he was riding into.

Chapter Four
Shadow

Shadow sat at the bar of the rundown establishment, he heard The Outlaws frequented. There were currently three of them sitting at a table in the corner. They had their cuts on, but he would have known them anywhere. They were drinking heavily, swearing loudly, and grabbing any girls ass that got close. The Outlaws were the kind of men that gave all bikers a bad name, and Shadow hated them on sight.

When the waitress refused to go anywhere near them anymore, one biker pushed out of the booth and headed for the bar. This was what Shadow had been hoping for. He had purposely sat at the end, so when the biker stopped, he ended up right beside.

"Shit waitress," Shadow said, as he tipped up his beer and took a sip.

The biker glanced in his direction. "Yeah, bitch won't come near the table." The bartender chose that moment to come over, and Shadow lost the biker's attention. The bartender filled the order and told the biker what he owed him.

"I got it," Shadow said, as he pulled out the money, and pushed it towards the bartender.

"Obliged," the biker responded. "Hammer," the biker introduced himself.

"Shade," Shadow told him, not wanting to give up his real name.

"Military," the biker asked.

"Ex Navy," he told him.

The biker nodded. "Join us for a drink", he asked, as he tilted his head towards the table. Shadow nodded and grabbed a couple beers to help carry them to the table.

Hammer introduced him to his buddies, Skull, Drake and Blade. The men were rough and crass. They spent the rest of the night drinking, laughing and talking about the women they'd banged. Shadow hated it all. It was getting late, and Shadow sensed the bikers were ready to leave.

"You got a place to crash," Hammer asked.

"Nah," Shadow said. "I was just gonna grab a room at the motel I saw off the highway."

"We got plenty of empty rooms at the clubhouse," Hammer invited. "You interested."

Shadow smirked. "I could crash there."

The men nodded and headed out, with Shadow following. They admired his Harley for a minute, then they were on their way. It surprised Shadow when they pulled up to a building surrounded by barbed wire.

"What is this place," Shadow asked. While they waited for a biker to open the gate.

"This used to be a correction facility for boys. Minors who were too young for jail, were at one time sent here. We bought it for a song about a year ago," Hammer told him proudly.

The gate opened, and the men rode through. They backed their bikes into a couple free spots in front of the building, then headed inside. The front room was huge and open. It looked like the men had built a bar across the back, and there were tables scattered all over the place.

"Who the fuck is that," a huge older biker asked, as he crossed the room and headed for them.

Hammer stepped forward then. "Bull, this is Shade. He's ex navy, and he's passing through. He didn't have a place to stay," he explained.

"You ever hear of The Outlaws before," Bull growled.

"Ran into some about a year ago, about six or eight hours south of here," he said. "They a chapter of your club," he asked.

Bull looked pissed. "That would have been my brothers club," he said. "A rival club took them out about six months ago."

"Fuck, sorry man," Shadow said. "That's rough."

Bull brushed him off with a wave of the hand. "Blood for blood," he said with a gleam in his eye. "The president killed my brother, so I took his sister. Pretty little thing," he smirked. "I tried to kill her, almost did too, but the girls got something about her. I decided that I'm making her mine instead. I think it will hurt the fucker more if he knows I'm banging her regularly."

"You got her here," Shadow asked in feigned surprise.

"Fuck ya," he said proudly. "You want to see her," Bull asked.

"Fuck ya," Shadow answered.

Bull laughed at his answer. "You're all right," he said. "We may have a spot for you here," he told him. Shadow hid his cringe.

Finally, things were coming together. But, Bull had mentioned almost killing her, so Shadow was worried about her condition. He followed Bull and Hammer up the stairs and thanked god he had gotten here when he did.

Chapter Five
Tiffany

Tiffany lay huddled on the bed in the small room. Her hands were tied together, and so were her feet, making it impossible to move. She had no idea how long she had been here, but she figured it was just under a week. She wanted to go home, but had a feeling she'd never see home again.

They took her from right outside her house. Tiffany had stepped outside for just a minute to get the mail, and she didn't even have time to blink it happened so fast. Two men jumped out from the side of the house and grabbed her. She fought, but they were strong. She was dragged to a van and thrown in the back.

She knew bikers had taken her because her brother was a biker. Preacher, as he liked to be called now, was the president of The Stone Knights. Preacher's father had been a biker too, and when he cheated on his wife, she was born. Of course, his wife had let him stay, so her and her mother were forgotten.

But Preacher had never forgotten her. He was eight years older, and when he had found out about her, at their father's funeral, he had been furious. He'd always wanted a sister, he'd told her. Her mother had hated her brother on sight deciding he was scum, like her father, but Preacher hadn't cared. He had called, visited, and given her presents and money all the time. She had fallen in love with her older brother instantly, and they became close.

Because bikers had taken her, she knew it had something to do with her brother, but she didn't blame him. His club was nothing but good, and she knew whatever reason he had, for doing whatever he had done, had been a good one. She just hoped her brother would deal okay with her death.

When they had first taken her and dumped her in this room, she had been unsure of what was happening. Then the president, Bull, had come in and sprouted nonsense about blood for blood. He had raped her, and afterwards had wrapped his hands around her neck and squeezed.

She felt for sure she would die, but then he had looked at her strangely. Suddenly, his hands were gone, and he was walking away, shutting the door behind him. Her throat had been on fire, and since that night, still was. If she tried to talk or scream, it bled. She was extremely weak too, having little to no food since the choking. Her throat hurt so bad she couldn't get down any of the food left for her. She had taken to just drinking water.

She also suffered bad headaches, but that was probably from him cutting off her oxygen for so long. Since then, he had come to sitting in the corner of her room for an hour each day, just watching her. It was creepy and freaked her out. She did not understand why he did it, but he hadn't touched her again, and she was grateful for that.

Tiffany still had on the dress she had been wearing at the time they took her, and it was badly torn. She tried to keep herself covered, but it was hard. They hadn't left her a blanket, and the room got cold at night.

She tried to fall asleep, but just as she was dozing off, the door opened. She glanced up as Bull walked in, then noticed a man following behind him. The man was taller than Bull and built like a football player. His hair was dark, and shaggy, and fell to his shoulders. Then she looked into his eyes and got lost. She couldn't look away, and she saw he was looking at her the same way.

Then Bull approached the bed, and her attention was pulled away from the new man. She cringed, as Bull ran his hand down her cheek. When she looked back at the other man, he was staring at her neck furiously. When he noticed her watching him, he masked his expression, then he winked at her.

She stared at him in confusion, then watched as the two men turned without a word and left the room, shutting the door behind them. She had no idea what had just happened.

Chapter Six
Shadow

Shadow had his hands shoved in his jeans pockets as he followed Bull up the stairs. The biker stopped at the end of the hall, at a door that had a prospect standing in front of it. Bull nodded at the prospect, then pushed the door open, and stepped inside. Shadow moved inside as well.

The room was small, and the only furnishings were a wooden chair in the corner, and a single bed that was pushed up against the wall. There was a window, but Shadow knew it was a two-story drop down. He took in everything, knowing he'd need it to make it out alive tonight.

Finally, he looked at the girl lying on the bed. His whole body froze as he stared at her. She was absolutely stunning. She looked tiny, lying on the single bed, so Shadow knew she was probably the same size as the women his brothers had. She had long light brown hair, that fell in soft waves around her, and her eyes were so blue, they reminded him of the ocean.

Then he pulled his gaze away and looked at the rest of her. He was furious when he saw the rope binding her arms and legs together. It was tied so tight that blood was pooled around it. Her dress was ripped so badly, that it barely covered her, and her arms and legs had some ugly looking bruises on them.

Suddenly, his eyes were drawn to her neck, and it was hard to hide the anger from his expression. The poor girl's neck was almost black all the way around, it was bruised so badly. And Shadow swore he could make out hand prints in the bruising. He knew without question that this was the way Bull had almost killed her.

When he looked into the girl's eyes again, he found her staring at him. She was hurt badly, and obviously terrified, but she held his stare. Wanting to ease her anxiety a bit, he winked at her. She looked back at him stunned, as Bull turned and headed back out the door. Without a backwards glance, Shadow turned as well and followed him, knowing if he looked back, he'd never be able to leave.

The girl lying on the bed was named Tiffany. Shadow had been told that by Preacher. He also had a picture in his wallet that Preached had given him, but it hadn't done her justice. She was way prettier, even with the state she was in.

But something about her drew him to her. It was almost like his heart had stopped, then started up again, when they locked eyes. It was taking everything he had, to walk away from her. He desperately wanted to pull out his gun and put a bullet between Bull's eyes. He knew without a doubt, he would move heaven and earth to save Tiffany tonight.

Bull moved down the stairs and headed right back to the bar. He grabbed a bottle of whiskey, and filled up a couple glasses, handing him one. Soon they were joined by Hammer.

"What did ya think of my girl Shade," Bull asked him.

"She's a bit of a mess," Shadow answered, hating to answer to the name Shade. The club didn't want him using his real road name.

"Oh, she'll heal. I fucked her up a bit when I strangled her. Probably should have decided to keep her, a bit quicker," he laughed. "My bad."

Shadow bit back the retaliation he wanted to growl and nodded at the biker.

"You like the look of things around here," Bull asked him curiously.

"You're definitely set up good, I like the guys I've met so far, and you certainly know how to have a good time," Shadow told him.

"Then I think you'd be a great addition to our club," Bull happily told him. "Let's get fucked up in celebration," Bull roared.

Four hours later, most of the bikers were stumbling to their beds drunk. Shadow acted drunk, as he headed to his assigned room, but he'd hardly drank at all. All night, as the bikers had done shot after shot, Shadow had been switching his full drinks with their empty ones.

Shadow pushed open the door and laid down on the bed. He'd allow himself two hours to rest, and then he was headed for the girl. She had been here too long already, it was time to get her out. He shot off a quick text to the brothers, letting them know he had found her, and would be on the move soon.

He pitied anyone that got in his way.

Chapter Seven
Shadow

Exactly two hours later, Shadow's eyes popped open. Being a Navy Seal, and used to waking up to take watch, his body pretty much automatically woke every two hours. He was hoping that after a time it would stop, but so far it hadn't. He climbed out of bed and grabbed his knapsack off the floor. It took him a minute to switch out his blue jeans, for black ones. He also put on a black hoodie, and a black skullcap. His hair was nearly black anyway, but he wasn't taking any chances.

He quietly opened the door and glanced in both directions. He saw two bikers passed out in the hall, but they both looked sound to the world. He stepped out, and headed down to the end where the stairs were. When he was almost to the top, he stopped, and got out a small gun that had a silencer on it. He wanted to take out every biker he saw, but the risk was too high that he'd end up shot. His priority was Tiffany.

He took the stairs and hurried to the top. The prospect was still standing outside the door at the end of the hall, dutifully following orders. Shadow moved down the hall silently, staying in the shadows like his training had taught him. When he was close enough, he took aim and fired. The shot hit the biker in the head, and Shadow had to hurry to catch him, as he fell.

Slowly he turned the knob on the door and dragged the dead biker inside. He sat him in the corner of the room on the floor, then quickly shut the door. So far he had been lucky, but that had been the easy part. He set his pack down and pulled out a knife he had hidden in his boot.

Finally, he turned to face Tiffany. She was in the exact same position she had been in earlier, which was a huge relief. It meant that none of the bikers had fucked with her. She was staring at his knife, and she was completely terrified. He got as close to the bed as he could, and crouched down, removing the knife from her line of sight. Her eyes instantly locked on his, and he felt that same rush as earlier. He knew he needed to be fast, so he decided to be blunt.

"Preacher sent me." The instant her brothers name left his lifts, her eyes widened. "I'm getting you out of here, and I'm taking you back to him," he whispered. "You with me?"

She nodded, but didn't say a word, as he brought the knife back up. He took hold of her wrists, and easily sliced through the rope, then did the same with her ankles. Blood dripped from the wounds, and he could see she was in obvious pain. He took a white t-shirt from his bag, and quickly ripped it into thin strips, which he then wrapped around each of the cuts. It certainly wouldn't help to leave a blood trail. Tiffany flinched, but again stayed quiet.

He moved to the window then and opened it. Peering out, he saw a biker standing below, but no one else was about. He pulled his gun back out and quickly took the man out. Then he grabbed the rope he had stashed in his pack and tied one end to the leg of the bed. He lifted Tiffany off the bed, and sat her in the chair, then silently moved the bed, so it was directly under the window. Once he was done, he knelt in front of the girl once more.

"We're going out the window," he told her. "There are too many men in the common room. You're going to need to climb on my back, and hold on as tight as you can," he told her. "I need my arms free to climb down, so I won't be able to hold you."

She nodded once, so he turned and tied his pack onto the end of the rope. Carefully, he lowered it to the ground, then he turned, so his back was to the girl. He waited patiently, hoping she would trust him, and climb on. After a minute, small hands wrapped around his neck, and he sighed in relief. It was time to get her out of here.

Chapter Eight
Tiffany

Tiffany had no idea what she was doing. The man had told her that her brother had sent him, but there was no proof. For some strange reason, she trusted him though, and right now her options were to go with him, or stay here. She definitely didn't want to stay here. After a minute, she wrapped her arms around his neck.

She flinched, when he grabbed both her legs, and brought them up, to wrap around his waist. He turned his head slightly, so his mouth was near her cheek. Then he startled her, by placing his lips softly against her cheek, and giving her a gentle kiss.

"Please don't ever be afraid of me Baby Girl," he begged. She couldn't respond even if she wanted to because the strangling had damaged her throat so bad. The only thing she could do, was to lay her head against his back. He nodded once, and she hoped that meant he understood. Then he rose, heading for the window.

Tiffany didn't have a lot of strength, but she held on with everything she could, as he climbed out the window, and sat on the sill. Then he turned and grabbed on to the rope. After a quick twist, he pushed away from the sill, and she closed her eyes in fright. She could feel him going hand over hand as he climbed to the ground.

He let go, and jumped the last bit, and she finally let out the breath she'd been holding, and opened her eyes. She started to let go, but he stopped her, placing his hand over hers.

"Stay where you are. I can move faster than you probably can, and with you on my back I'll know exactly where you are," he whispered. She tightened her grip again and settled back against him.

He took off then, moving quickly, as he rounded the building. She couldn't see anything, but she could hear the quiet click, each time he fired his gun. He moved fast, and she held perfectly still, not wanting to distract him.

Suddenly, someone grabbed her around the waist, and pulled her off him. She struggled as the man tightened his hold. She couldn't cry out, but at least she knew it wasn't Bull who had her. She watched as the man rescuing her fired at two men in front of them, killing them instantly. Slowly, he turned back to face her, and his eyes widened.

"Who the fuck are you," the man holding her roared. Tiffany looked around, afraid his yelling would bring others, but no one came.

"Put her down Hammer," he growled, as he raised his weapon and aimed at them.

"Fuck you Shade. I brought you in, you were gonna be one of us. I'd bet my fucking life, you're one of those god damned Stone Knights pussies," he sneered.

Tears flowed down her face as she realized the biker wasn't going to let her go. She knew Shade, as the biker had called him, didn't have a shot. Hammer was using her as a shield. She twisted and turned, scratching at his arms, with everything she had left.

She watched as Shade lowered his gun and fired. Hammer suddenly dropped her, and she hit the cement hard. She looked back to see him grab his foot as he rolled on the ground screaming.

"Eyes on me Baby Girl," Shade yelled. She quickly looked back at him, to see him fire three quick shots in Hammers's direction.

He hurried back to her, and in a move of pure strength, picked her up, and twisted her so she was on his back again. She plastered herself against him and held tight. He ran again, and she prayed they made it out safely. In a few short minutes, Shade was proving to be her saviour, and she needed one right now.

Chapter Nine
Shadow

Shadow only encountered one more person as he hurried to his bike. He knew most of the bikers were asleep, or passed out, which is why he waited so long before making a move. Finally, he made it to the bike. He crouched down and whispered to Tiffany.

"Hop down baby girl," he ordered.

Shadow waited a minute, then her legs dropped from his waist, and her small arms slid from his neck. He turned quickly, to see her trying to cover herself with her torn dress. Unzipping his black hoodie, he shrugged out of it, then held it up as she slipped her arms into it. He hurried to zip it up, then rolled up the sleeves, so her hands were free.

Picking her up, he gently set her down on the seat, then kicked the kickstand with his foot. Grunting, he pushed the beast of a bike, as he made his way as close to the gatehouse as he could. He stopped near some trees and put the kickstand down again. Then he turned to look at Tiffany again.

"I need to go take out the guard, and get that gate open," he told her. "You stay here. I'll be able to see you, and I'll only be a minute."

She nodded, but he could tell she really didn't want to be left alone. Her eyes were huge, and her gaze was darting everywhere at once. He kissed her cheek again, then took off through the trees. Thankfully, only one guard was waiting at the gate, and he was the same one that was there when he came in.

Shadow rapped on the door, and the idiot came right over and opened it. He grabbed the bikers head and slammed it into the door jam. The biker fell to the ground. Shadow knew he was running out of time, so he ran straight back to his bike. Tiffany looked terrified, but thankfully she was still perched on his bike waiting.

He knocked up the kickstand, and pushed the bike down the lane, and through the gate. Then once more he stopped and knocked the kickstand down again. He darted back to the gatehouse and headed inside. It took only a second to find the switch to open and close the gate. He slammed the palm of his hand down on it and was satisfied when the gate started to close. Once he was sure it was tight, he crouched down low, and reached under the console, to rip out every wire he could find.

Satisfied, no one was getting the gate open for a while, he moved to the unconscious man, and pulled off his leather vest. He tossed it over his shoulder, the left the gatehouse, and moved to the gate itself. He grabbed a hold of the side and quickly started to climb. When he reached the top, he threw the vest over the barbed wire, and continued climbing. In seconds, he was on the ground beside his bike.

Poor Tiffany was swaying as she sat there looking up at him. He grabbed her shoulders to steady her and knew instantly that she probably wouldn't be able to hold on. He looked down at his hoodie and got an idea. The first thing he did was place a helmet on her head. Then he pushed the bike down the road for about five minutes. After all the trouble he went to trying to be quiet, he didn't need the rumble of his bike, waking anyone up.

When he was satisfied he had pushed it a safe distance, he moved back to Tiffany. She looked awful. Her neck was a mess, her dress was flapping in the wind where the hoodie didn't cover it, and she was covered in cuts and bruises, but she sat there looking up at him expectantly. Shadow admired her strength.

"We have a long way to ride," he told her, as he unrolled the sleeves, he had rolled up a few minutes ago. "Do you think you can hold on?"

Tiffany looked at him with determination, but then she deflated as she slowly shook her head no. He saw a tear run down her cheek and knew she really wanted to say yes. It probably hurt her to admit that. He brushed away the tear, then climbed on in front of her.

First, he lifted her legs, and wrapped them around his waist, tucking her cold bare feet under his thighs. Next, he grabbed her arms and pulled them around him, tying the ends of the hoodie together.

"Now you can't fall off," he told her, as he started the bike and tore off down the deserted road.

Chapter Ten
Tiffany

Tiffany was having a hard time staying conscious. Her arms and legs hurt, where the ropes had torn them, her head throbbed, her throat was on fire, and she was hungry and thirsty. She had no idea how long they had been on the bike, but she knew it couldn't have been long.

She started to doze, and even with the hoodie tied, she still leaned dangerously to the side. She couldn't call out because of her damaged throat, and she was terrified of what was about to happen. Suddenly, the biker in front of her twisted his arm back, and grabbed the side of the hoodie, preventing her from slipping further.

She sighed in relief, as he slowed, and pulled the bike to the shoulder of the road. They were in the middle of nowhere, the country road was small and deserted. She could feel him untying the hoodie, and then her legs were lowered. He kept a hold of her with one hand as he twisted and looked back at her.

"You done for a bit baby girl," he asked, as he searched her face. She slumped in defeat as she nodded at him. "Can you talk at all," he asked, as he looked at her throat. She shook her head no at him, and he growled. Her eyes shot up to his in fright as his expression morphed into pure anger.

"Don't be afraid of me," he told her again. "I'm angry about what was done to you, not at you," he explained. "Are you cold," he asked, and she nodded immediately.

"We don't have a lot of time, but I have clothes in my bag that should fit you. Can you stay seated for a minute," he asked in concern. Again she could only nod at him.

She watched as he climbed off, and went to the saddlebags, opening one and pulling out a small bag. He then produced what looked like yoga pants and a t-shirt, from inside. He set them on his seat, then took her right leg and lifted it over the bike, so she was sitting sideways on the seat. He lifted the yoga pants and placed one leg gently in at a time. When he had them pulled up to her knees, he lifted her easily, and set her on the ground.

She watched him for a minute, but he only helped her stand upright. A tear left her eye as she realized he was waiting for her to pull them up the rest of the way. Thank you, she mouthed to him, before quickly pulling them up. He then helped her take off the hoodie and turned his back as he handed her the t-shirt. It was difficult, with her wrists so bad, but she got it on.

When she tapped him on the shoulder, he turned back, and handed her a sweatshirt. She could see it was a girl's, but she shook her head and pointed to his again. He smiled at her, and never said a word, just picked up his sweatshirt and helped her put it back on. Then he lifted her up and sat her back on the seat. He placed socks on her feet, carefully pulling them up over the makeshift bandages, and then slipped on running shoes.

She was so warm and comfy, she sighed. Then she looked at him and mouthed, thank you Shade. He lost his smile and frowned at her.

"Names Shadow," he told her. "I used Shade, so they wouldn't know my name." He paused for a minute and studied her. "We need to move again, as we've got further to go tonight. Can you ride for another hour before we break again for a bit." She looked up at him slightly unsure, but she nodded anyway.

Suddenly, he picked her up, and she wrapped her arms and legs around him automatically. The next thing she knew, he was straddling the bike, with her on his lap. Slightly uneasy, she leaned back, and looked up at him in question.

"You won't make it another hour, and I can't wait. This way I can hold you with one arm, and I'll know you're safe. It's all back roads, so no one will stop us," he explained. "I promise I won't let you fall."

She said nothing, just snuggled close, stealing his warmth, and laid her head on his shoulder. She had no idea why she trusted him so fast, but she wouldn't question it. She was sure she heard him whisper, that's my girl, before he cranked the bike and took off.

Chapter Eleven
Shadow

Shadow held the girl as close to his chest as he could. She was cold, and she was hurt, and he had no idea how she wasn't a sobbing mess. Maybe it was the adrenaline rush, and once they stopped, she'd break. Bull was a dead man when he saw him again, what he had done to the girl was inhuman.

He continued down the road, getting closer to Sniper. He hoped that by taking back roads, The Outlaws wouldn't find them. He knew he was being unrealistic, but maybe they'd stick to the highways first. Shadow had bought them some time, but he needed more. The girl needed rest and medical attention, and he needed to make time for that.

Finally, he saw one small light in the distance, and knew right away it was Sniper. One light could only mean it was a motorcycle, and it wasn't moving. Shadow didn't relax though, knowing the bikers couldn't be too far behind him. He pushed his bike faster and pulled up beside his best friend a minute later. Sniper smiled over at him, and he couldn't help but smile back.

"Thank fuck you made it out," Sniper said, in obvious relief. "You have any trouble?"

"Some," Shadow admitted. "But nothing I couldn't handle. I jammed the gate when I left, but I'm sure they won't be too far behind me," he told him. "You find somewhere close we can go? The girl needs medical attention, rest and food," he told his friend.

"Yep, there's a cabin up ahead, and it looks like the owners are away. If we go to a motel, they'll find us for sure, so it's our best bet," he said. "We can call the brothers from there."

"Lead the way," Shadow said, agreeing with him. Sniper turned his bike around and took off down the road. Shadow kissed Tiffany on the head and took off after him. The only indication she was awake, was when she tightened her grip on the back of his t-shirt. She didn't move once during the whole conversation, so Sniper hadn't gotten a good look at her.

He watched as Sniper slowed, then took a small dirt road up ahead. Shadow slowed as well, then made the same turn his brother had. He was glad the road was packed dirt and not gravel. Gravel always messed up the paint job on a bike, the tiny rocks getting kicked up in the air scratched like crazy.

After a couple turns, Sniper stopped in front of a small cabin. Shadow pulled in beside him and shut off his bike. Then he lowered his head as he wrapped both his arms around Tiffany.

"We're stopping here for a rest. The man with us is Sniper, and he's a friend of your brothers and mine. I need to check you over, and I need to fix up those wounds," he told her. "Can you walk baby girl, or am I carrying you?"

He felt her loosen her arms and legs, but then tense up, so he decided for her. He slung his leg over the bike and stood, taking her with him. She relaxed back against him, and he was glad, he liked holding her. He moved to the cabin, and Sniper had the door open already. Shadow nodded at his brother as he walked through. He headed straight for the couch and laid her down. A minute later, Sniper was beside him.

"How bad," his brother asked quietly.

"Bad," Shadow told him, as he pushed the hair out of her face, which had covered her neck.

"Fuck," Sniper said, and he knew the brother had gotten a good look. Sniper then moved out of Tiffany's line of sight and mouthed the word rape to him. Shadow could only nod sadly. Then Sniper turned on his heal, said something about getting the bags, and went back out the door. Shadow knew his brother was pissed, and had left so he could calm down, and he appreciated that. When he looked down again, Tiffany was looking up at him.

"I'm gonna fix you up baby girl," he told her. "You're gonna be just fine," he promised, as he stroked her hair. "And I'm gonna make sure of it."

Chapter Twelve
Tiffany

Tiffany watched, as Sniper brought in a couple bags, and set them on the floor. After routing through them, he handed a medical kit to Shadow. Shadow moved back to her and sat on the floor.

"Can you see if there's any soup in the kitchen, that we can heat. Tiffany probably can't get anything down that's solid," he told Sniper. When Sniper looked over to her, she nodded in agreement. He smiled, then headed away to see what he could find.

"I'm pretty sure this will hurt baby girl," he told her, as he lifted her arm and removed one of the makeshift bandages. It wasn't too bad, except in the places where the dried blood had stuck it to the skin. He was quick at cleaning it, applying an ointment, and replacing the bandage with gauze and a proper wrap. He did that to her other wrist, and then the same to her ankles.

When he was done, he looked at her throat. It was bruised extremely badly, and the inside looked raw, he told her.

"Can you get anything down," he asked.

"Liquid," she mouthed to him.

"Did he do this as soon as he took you," he asked. She nodded in agreement.

"Okay," he said. "There are a ton of muscles in the neck. I'm pretty sure he damaged several of them when he strangled you. If that's all it is, then you should heal, but we'll need a doctor and some X-rays before we know for sure," he explained.

She raised an eyebrow at him in question, wondering how he knew all that. He smiled at her then.

"I was a Navy Seal. In basic training we're taught basic field medicine, because sometimes we're hurt and there's no one to help us. Sniper was a marine, so he had some medical training." Suddenly, a pad and paper was set down beside her.

"Found it in a drawer," Sniper said. "Soup will be ready in a minute." Then he turned and left as quietly as he had come.

Is that why you were the one to come get me, she wrote on the pad. Then she flipped it around so he could read it.

"I volunteered," he told her. "With my training, I knew I was your best choice." She nodded at him, then looked down. Warm fingers on her chin tilted it back up. "I'm glad I came baby girl," he told her. "There's no place I'd rather be."

He held her eyes for a minute, then looked away, as Sniper placed a bowl of soup in front of her. Both him and Shadow had their own bowl of soup, along with some sandwiches. She greedily slurped at the soup, happy to have something in her belly. It hurt to swallow, but it was so good, she didn't care.

Sniper cleaned away the bowls, and when he came back, he had a cell in his hand. "Preacher wants to talk to you," he said. "He knows you can't talk, but he wants you to listen." She nodded, so he handed her the phone.

Preacher's voice caused tears to run down her cheeks. "Hey little sister," he said quietly. "I'm so glad you made it out okay. You can trust the men I sent to you, they'll bring you safely to me. I wanted to come, but the brothers told me I couldn't bring the dynamite, so I stayed back." She smiled at that one. "You're gonna be okay. The brothers will get you here, and you're gonna stay with me for a while. I'm so sorry sis," he said as his voice broke. "This is all my fault."

She closed her eyes in anguish, her big brother never broke, but here he was, breaking while he was talking to her.

"Not your fault," she whispered into the phone. Then cringed at the pain it caused.

He was quiet for a minute. "You listen to the men," he then ordered. "You do everything they tell you, and you stay safe", he practically roared into the phone. "I love you," he growled.

"Love you too," she forced out. Then the phone was taken off of her. Shadow swiped at something on her lip as he angrily handed the phone back to Sniper. When he showed her, she was surprised to see blood on his finger.

"No more talking for you," he demanded. "You want a shower," he asked. She nodded immediately, at the thought of getting clean. "Sniper, see if there's any Saran Wrap in the kitchen," he yelled. She blinked at him, not understanding why he'd need Saran Wrap.

Chapter Thirteen
Shadow

Shadow covered Tiffany's wrists and ankles in Saran Wrap, so they wouldn't get wet. Then he watched as she went into the bathroom and shut the door. He really felt for her and hoped she would be alright. In the short amount of time he had known her, he knew already, that he was falling for her.

"Staring at the door will not make her come out faster," Sniper said, from his position on the couch.

Shadow just turned his head and glared at his best friend. When he heard the shower start up, he turned and headed for the couch as well, practically falling onto it.

"You already have feelings for the girl," Sniper observed.

"Yeah," Shadow admitted. "But she's been through a lot, and it's not over yet. Now isn't the time for that."

"Nope, and I don't envy you. But you can't tell your heart when to fall in love. Besides, that girl in there," he said as he pointed to the bathroom. "she needs you right now."

"Yeah," Shadow said again. "But I think I need her too." Then he changed the topic. "So what's the plan, Tiffany needs rest. She's having a hard time staying on the bike. She's tired, she's hurt, and I don't think they gave her anything she could eat. She's not going to make it much longer," he admitted.

"Right," Sniper said. "Preacher's loosing it. I told him about the strangling and warned him it looked like they raped her. He's probably torn up the entire clubhouse by now."

Shadow stared at his brother, pissed he went into such detail. "Why the fuck would you tell him that," he asked.

"He needs to get over it before she gets there. She's gonna need her brother, and he can't go off pissed in front of her," Sniper said.

"Fuck, okay," Shadow agreed. "What about the brothers," he asked.

"They're still waiting for us down the road. I'm thinking, when she gets out of the bathroom, I go scope the area while she rests. I don't want to be heading out with her, only to ride right into trouble."

Shadow nodded at him as he heard the shower shut off. "That sounds good, but you better be careful. Bull will have the whole club looking for us, and you don't want to be caught out there on your own."

Sniper smirked at him. "They won't see me," he said with complete confidence. "Go check on your girl, while I head out," he ordered.

Shadow watched as his brother headed out the door, then he headed for the bathroom. He knocked on the door and waited, but Tiffany never opened up.

Finally, he pushed the door open, and walked inside. Tiffany was dressed and staring at her neck in the mirror. She wasn't crying, but she looked so sad it broke his heart. He spun her around, and pulled her tight to his chest, she immediately clung to him.

"It will be okay baby girl. You're gonna heal, and you're gonna be all right. I'll be by your side, and I'll help you," he promised.

Then he took her hand and led her to one of the bedrooms. He helped tuck her in and told her to get some rest. She looked so small in the big bed, but he closed over the door, and left the room. He really wanted to stay, but he didn't want to push her.

Ten minutes later, the door opened again, and out she came. She picked up her pen and paper, and wrote something down, then handed it to him. I want to stay close to you. I'm not scared when you're there, the note said. He nodded, and moved to the end of the chesterfield, motioning to her to lay down. She did so, without wasting a second, laying her head on his lap.

He hoped she knew with each gesture she made, she was becoming his. And once she was, there was no way he was letting her go.

Chapter Fourteen
Shadow

Exactly two hours later, Sniper was pushing back through the door. Shadow sat up straighter and nodded at his brother. He had tried to get a bit of sleep, knowing he would need it. He looked down to see Tiffany stirring as well. She slowly opened her eyes, and when she looked up and saw him watching her, a small smile spread across her face.

"You should keep sleeping," he told her, as he smiled down at her. He pushed the hair off her face and ran his finger down her cheek. She shook her head no, and sat up, but he was happy to see that she stayed close.

Sniper moved towards them and placed a paper bag on the coffee table. He reached inside, and pulled out a straw, setting it on the table.

"My sister Misty got really sick once," he said. "Her throat was so swelled up, it was hard to swallow. The doctor told us to give her boost. It's a meal replacement drink. It would give her all the nutrients her body needed, and it would fill her up," he told them. Then he pulled out a can, opened it, and placed the straw in it.

"It's chocolate," he said, as he handed it to her. "That was my sisters favourite." Shadow watched as she took the drink from Sniper and tried some. Her face lit up, and she smiled at him, making Shadow instantly jealous. Thank you, she mouthed to him.

Sniper nodded at her, then turned to Shadow. "The Outlaws are everywhere out there. We may get through, but it will be difficult. I don't really want to take any chances," he told him.

Shadow nodded for a minute, then picked up his cell. He hit a button, then waited a minute. Steele picked up on the third ring.

"Shadow, where are you," the brother asked.

"Still at the cabin," he told him. "Sniper says The Outlaws patrol the roads heavily. We need a way out. You think you can rent a cube van. You can get up here without being noticed, and we can hide the bikes and ourselves in the back."

"Can do," Steele told him. "It'll take a couple hours. You safe where you are?"

"Should be," Shadow told him. "Can you track my phone," he asked.

"Definitely," Steele said. "Hang tight brother." Then he hung up.

"Smart," Sniper said. "I think that just may work."

Shadow smirked, hoping it would. He looked at Tiffany, and saw she was still curled up beside him, sucking on her drink. With her shower, soup and now boost in her, she was looking better. Her colour was coming back, and she was perking up.

"A couple hours baby girl," he told her. "Then we're back on the road to your brother. I suggest you get a couple more hours sleep. The rest will help," he told her.

"I'll take the chair," Sniper said. "I'll hear them before they turn down the lane." The brother then stretched out in the arm chair, propping his feet up on the coffee table. He laid his head back, crossed his arms over his chest, and closed his eyes.

Shadow stood Tiffany up, then laid down on the chesterfield, placing his back tight to the back. He held out his hand to her and was thrilled when a second later she placed her tiny hand in his. He pulled her down until she was laying with her back tight to his chest. He placed her head on his arm and rested his chin against it.

Shadow waited a minute to see what she would do. A second later, she slid her hand back into his, and pulled it tight to her stomach. In another minute he heard her breathing even out and knew she was asleep.

He glanced over to Sniper, to see he was wide awake. The brother winked at him, then closed his eyes again. Shadow smiled slightly, then closed his eyes too. Things were about to get damn complicated.

Chapter Fifteen
Tiffany

Tiffany woke to Shadow gently stroking her face and calling her name. She blinked a couple times, then stared up at him. He was a handsome man, and she knew she was falling for him. She just hoped that he felt the same way. She really wanted to see him again when this was all over.

"The trucks here baby girl, it's time to go," he told her. He helped her sit, and it was then she heard doors shutting, and feet pounding on the gravel.

"You're sure it's your club," she wrote on her pad. Fearful that it may not be.

"God dammit Shadow, get out here. Trike and Dagger brought dynamite," Sniper yelled from outside.

She watched as Shadow chuckled, and his face lit up. "Yeah, those are my brothers," he said. "Come meet them." Then he was hauling her up, and heading for the door, towing her along behind him. She was a little unsure, but this was her brother's friends, and they were all here because of him.

Shadow stopped at the bottom of the porch steps. The truck was bigger than she expected, but it had a moving company logo on the side, and a pullout ramp they had already lowered.

"Hey brother, glad to see your safe," one biker said as he approached. He gave Shadow a half hug, and a pound on the back, while she watched from behind them. When they broke apart, Shadow pulled her hand, so she came forward and tucked her into his side.

"I'll like you to meet Preachers little sister Tiffany," he told the whole group. She shyly gave them a half smile. They were huge men and together were a bit intimidating.

Shadow pointed out the man he had hugged first. "Baby girl this is Steele. He's your brothers Vice President." Steele smiled down at her.

"Nice to meet you honey," he said quietly, instantly putting her at ease.

"Then there's Dragon, Navaho, Trike, Raid and Dagger," Shadow told her, as to pointed to each man. They had each smiled and nodded at her as their name was mentioned. It transformed them from scary bikers to scary teddy bears.

Tiffany watched as Dagger stepped forward and reached for her hand. She shied away and moved further into Shadow's body. She was still scared after her experience with The Outlaws. Dagger didn't seem fazed at all, just dropped his hand, and kept smiling.

"Preacher never told us how pretty you were," he said. "They must have been crazy to let an angel like you out of heaven."

She blinked up at him, not having a clue what to say, then she heard the growling start beside her. Immediately Sniper was beside her, pulling her away from Shadow.

"Let's stand over here a minute, shall we," he said. Then she watched, as Shadow launched himself at Dagger, and took him to the ground. Steele moved to stand on her other side when the bikers rolled too close to his feet.

"It's like that is it," Steele asked Sniper, and she watched as Sniper nodded back.

"I think she's his one," Sniper told him. Confused, she looked up at Sniper, but then heard Shadow bellow from the ground.

"Yes, she's my one. Now both of you get the fuck away from her," he snarled, as he pushed Dagger away from him and stood up. "And no more cheesy pick up lines Don Juan," he yelled down at the biker. Then he marched over to her and pulled her back into his side. She curled in and looked up at him.

"What do you mean, I'm your one," she mouthed to him.

"It means Preachers gonna kill him," Sniper said. "He just declared you as his," he explained.

She looked back up at Shadow, wanting him to say something else. He sighed, then placed his palm on her cheek.

"It means, that the first time I saw you, my heart literally stopped. I'm falling hard and fast for you. I can't explain it, other than to say I'm drawn to you, and need to have you close all the time," he told her.

She stared up at him as tears rolled down her cheeks. Not knowing what to do, because she couldn't talk, she threw herself at him. He caught her and held her close. She felt the same way, and she was over the moon he did too. She leaned back and mouthed me too to him, and his smile made her heart flutter.

"Well this just got interesting," Dragon said. "Come on brothers, we have a funeral to organize," he said as he moved back to the truck.

Chapter Sixteen
Shadow

The first thing the brothers did, was load up the bikes. The moving truck had hooks in the ceiling and walls, so it was easy to wrap straps around the bikes, and secure them. Shadow's and Sniper's bikes were the only two, the rest of the brothers had ridden in the back of the truck. Apparently, they left their bikes at the motel they were staying at, and Mario's men were getting a trailer and heading up to grab them.

Shadow felt much more secure, knowing he was heading back with the brothers. If he needed backup, he now had it. The brothers also packed quite a bit of firepower, so they were ready for anything. But he wasn't surprised to see the dynamite sitting in a box in the corner.

They decided Dragon and Sniper would sit in the front. Dragon had no fear, and was the best driver in dangerous situations, whereas Sniper was the deadliest shot. The two of them were their best bet. The rest of the brothers would ride in the back. The floor wouldn't be that comfortable, but they'd all be hidden away. If they ran into trouble, they'd open the back doors, and fire from there.

The boys had already thought things out and had purchased some huge pieces off steel. Once the bikes were loaded, they attached the steel to the inside of the truck, about a foot from the doors. This would give both the bikes, and the brothers protection. If a shootout happened, they now had cover.

Finally, they were ready to head out. There was a light turned on in the back of the truck, and all the brothers sat down and leaned against the side. Tension was high, and the brothers were quiet. It would be a good four or five hour drive, and it would be pretty boring.

Shadow sat near the front, with Tiffany curled up between his legs. She was terrified, and he was trying to give her some comfort. The truck rolled along, and the vibration was a killer on their asses. He could tell Tiffany was expecting the worst, and he couldn't seem to get her to relax. He could feel her shaking in his arms.

"When I went to war, it terrified me," he told her. "Sure I'd had lots of training, but it wasn't like being in the field. The adrenaline rush, the need to do something, it gets to you. What I used to do, is grab hold of my dog tags and hold on. They grounded me and made me remember the reasons why I was there."

He pulled them out of his shirt and lifted them over his head. She was staring at them in fascination when he carefully placed them over her head. She shook her head and try to give them back, so he placed his hands over hers.

"As long as you have these, you never have to worry. They're a part of me, and I'll always be with you. I've got your life in my hands, and I won't let you down," he vowed.

She stared up at him a minute as tears leaked from her cheeks. Then she turned and got on her her knees. She placed her small hand on his chest and pushed up. Shadow was shocked, when she placed her soft lips against his own, and kissed him. He moved his hand to the back of her head and held her there. He kept the kiss light and soft, not wanting to frighten her, and was relieved when she relaxed into him.

After a minute, he pulled away, and smiled down at her. She had the dog tags in her hand and she was clinging to them. Thank you, she mouthed to him, then she sat back down.

When he looked to his brothers, they were all wiping at their eyes, brushing away imaginary tears.

"That was just beautiful," Dagger said, then all the brothers laughed.

"Fucking bikers," Shadow said, as he pulled Tiffany closer.

Then all hell broke loose as someone fired shoots at the truck.

Chapter Seventeen
Shadow

At the first sign of gunshots, Shadow was up and pushing Tiffany into the corner, yelling at her to stay down. The truck walls were thick, and the bullets weren't penetrating, but it still had Shadow worried. He moved to the small panel that separated the back of the truck from the driver and slid it open. His brothers were already loading up and preparing for the battle. As soon as the window opened, Sniper was yelling.

"Eight bikes. Two in front, two more on either side, and two in the rear. We can try to swerve to take out the ones on the sides, but it's gonna get rough for a few minutes," Sniper yelled, as he pulled a rifle up off the floor. "I'll get the two in the front."

"Do it," he roared, then he turned to his brothers in the back with him. "It's gonna get rough, hold on to something," he shouted, then he dove for Tiffany, and pulled her in his arms. His body was surrounding hers, and now he would take the brunt of any hits.

She was shaking and crying, but there was nothing he could say, to take away her fear. The truck swerved left and right as it bumped along the road. He could still hear the bullets impacting the sides and Sniper's bullets going off in the front.

"One down in front, one on either side," Sniper yelled. "Two moved to the back, so that's five back there. Get those god damned doors open and fire," he ordered.

Steele moved quickly, releasing the latch, and kicking open the doors, then he dove behind the steel guard, as Raid and Trike fired. In seconds he was beside them, firing as well. They surprised the Outlaws, and before they could react, they hit two. Bikes went flying, and the three remaining men swerved, avoiding the wreckage.

Dagger was at the side reloading. "Dagger, I'm a Seal," Shadow yelled. "I'm a good shot, I need to help."

"You stay where the fuck you are," his brother yelled back. "Anything happens to Preachers sister, this will seem like child's play."

"Two four by fours are heading our way," Steele shouted, as he kept firing. "The bikes are backing off, and the vehicles are getting fucking close."

"Grab something, and brace," Dragon yelled. Shadow tucked Tiffany's head in close to his chest and reached for the hook in the floor closest to him.

Suddenly, Dragon slammed on the brakes, and both the vehicles crashed into the back of the truck. One was struck, ending up slightly under the back of the truck, but the other reversed and backed off. The truck that was wedged underneath was an easy target, and the brothers fired off quick shots, killing the two men inside.

"Go," Trike yelled, as he aimed and fired at the retreating four by four.

"Tires," Shadow yelled, "aim for the tires." The bikers nodded, and aimed lower, firing again.

Shadow raised his head so he could see, and was in time to watch as the front right tire blew, and the four by four flipped. Raid aimed then and fired a single shot at the vehicle. Instantly it exploded, sending a ball of flame into the sky.

"The bikes are retreating," Steele yelled. "Let's get the hell out of here. Everyone okay," he roared.

"We're fine up here," Sniper yelled from the front.

"We're good," Shadow yelled, after taking a quick look at Tiffany. "Drive for about five minutes, then pull over so we can close these fucking doors," he ordered Dragon.

"Right," Dragon yelled back.

Shadow pulled Tiffany up and wiped the tears from her face. "It's okay baby girl, I got you," he soothed. She glanced at each biker she could see, then turned back to Shadow. Okay she mouthed.

"Yeah, okay," Shadow agreed. Then she burst into tears again and threw herself into his arms. He held her as she let it out while the brothers looked on sympathetically.

"You think they'll give us our deposit back," Dagger asked seriously. The brothers snickered, and Shadow was happy to see Tiffany even had a half smile on her face. Leave it to Dagger to think of that he thought.

Chapter Eighteen
Shadow

Fifteen minutes later, they were on the road again, after their stop to close the doors. The brothers reloaded their guns, and got everything ready again, in case they needed it. They still had a couple hours to go. This time though, Dragon was really pushing it, he was headed for the compound, and they all wanted to get behind the safety of the gates.

Tiffany had calmed down after her break and was doing surprisingly well. Shadow kept her wrapped up in his arms, and she held onto him, and the dog tags. He was glad he gave them to her. The brothers all had their heads back, and their eyes closed, knowing they needed to rest while they could.

They were about forty minutes out when they were woken by Dragon slamming on the brakes. The men went flying around the back, crashing into each other and the walls.

"What the fuck," Steele roared, as he pulled himself up off the floor.

"You better take a look at this," Dragon yelled from the cab. All the brothers stood and hurried to the small window, peering out to the road ahead of them. Shadow stood, pulling Tiffany up with him, so they could see too.

"Fuck me, we're fucked," Raid said from over Shadow's shoulder.

"I'm a good shot, but they'll get us before I can get all of them," Sniper said.

Ahead of them, were two four by fours parked across the road. The road was a county road, and not wide, so the four by fours did an excellent job of blocking the way. In front of the vehicles were six men, and they were all holding guns. Of course, they pointed all the guns at the truck.

"Any suggestions," Dragon hollered.

Tiffany started hitting all their arms, to get their attention, and finally they turned to look at her. Let me go, she mouthed to them, as tears streamed down her cheeks. They want me, she continued.

"And you think they're gonna let us just drive away after they have you", Trike questioned. "Honey, they'll gun us down. Not to mention you were in the back with us, and they didn't seem to be too careful before," he told her.

Tiffany slumped her shoulders in defeat, and Shadow kissed her head. Dagger moved away and rifled through a box.

"Now can we use the dynamite," he asked, like a kid in a candy store, as he held some up.

"Fuck me," Steele said, as he walked over to him. "Fucking right we can use the dynamite," he roared.

"Sniper how's your pitching arm," Raid asked from the back. "Still got that wicked fast ball."

"You bet your ass, pass it up brothers," he hollered back. Dagger passed two bundles to Steele, who then passed it through the window to Sniper.

"Hold the fuck on, and watch your heads, this is gonna get ugly," Dragon roared, as he stepped on the gas and floored it. Sniper rolled down the window and waited until they got closer.

When The Outlaws saw they were headed straight for them, bullets flew. Shadow protected Tiffany as best he could, but everyone stayed at the window, not wanting to miss a thing. Bullets flew off the front of the truck and the windshield, shattering the glass, and barely missing Dragon and Sniper.

Suddenly, Sniper lit the fuze, then leaned out the side window, and chucked the dynamite right at the bikers in front.

"Mother fucker," he yelled, as he pulled in a bloody arm. But his aim was true, and it blew the bikers and their four by fours to pieces. He lit the second one and threw it anyway, then they all braced, as Dragon plowed right through the fire and wreckage.

Dragon and Trike were giving each other high fives, and whooping it up, as Dragon barrelled on down the road.

"Craziest bunch of bikers I've ever met," Raid said, as he smirked at them all, and shock his head. "But this is the best day I've had in ages," he admitted.

"Welcome to the Knights," Steele said, as he thumped him on the back. "We aim to please."

Chapter Nineteen
Tiffany

Tiffany couldn't believe The Outlaws were this persistent. First the motorcycles chased them, then the four by fours joined in, and then they made a roadblock. She had thought the bikers were kidding when they mentioned the dynamite, but apparently not. The bikers were crazy, but they were holding strong, and almost to the compound. These men were tough, she thought.

She had been concerned about Sniper and had made them stop. Raid had checked his arm and declared the bullet just grazed him. The wound had bled a lot, but the biker would be fine. It was cleaned and bandaged, and Tiffany was relieved.

Now they were headed back to the compound and had about twenty minutes to go. Shadow still held her, and she was grateful. She glanced over and saw Steele was on the phone.

"Tripp, we got Preacher's sister, but we've run into some trouble on the way back," the man paused. "What dynamite," he said. "Fine, can you cover it up? Good, appreciated. Keep your eyes on things and listen. Any sign of the bikers, you gotta let me know. Right." Then the man hung up.

"Tripp's gonna keep an ear to the ground, and he's gonna clean up the mess we left behind," he said. "Fuckers getting more crooked by the minute. I really think he hates his job. Maybe we should recruit him," Steele said.

"Then who the fucks gonna look after us," Dagger asked. Tiffany looked around to see nobody answered. They all looked confused.

Suddenly, they were surrounded by sleek black cars. Terrified, Tiffany clung to Shadow again. But Dragon was hanging out the window as he drove and yelling down at someone.

"Mario, what the fuck are you doing here," he bellowed.

"Heard you were blowing shit up. Didn't want to miss it," Tiffany heard yelled back.

"Right," Dragon yelled. "You got firepower."

"We're packing," the man responded.

Then the cars literally surrounded the truck as it crawled the last few miles to the compound. Tiffany had learned the bullets had done a lot of damage. The engine was smoking badly, and it was surprising they still moved. The windshield had been struck twice, so the bikers had kicked it out, and left it on the side of the road. One tire was riding on the rim, and the back door was tied shut. Apparently, the four by fours had bent it, when they impacted with the back.

The men were silent on the last leg as they hunkered down and sat by themselves. Tiffany figured they had to be tired, but they were holding strong, and still prepared for anything.

"You excited to see your brother baby girl," Shadow asked her. She nodded at him. It had been awhile since she'd last seen him, and she couldn't wait to have her big brother just hold her. She knew everything would be better once they were together.

"He really lost it, when he found out they took you," Shadow told her quietly. "He's gonna be over protective for a while," he told her.

She nodded at him, she was looking forward to a little over protectiveness for a while. Then she stood, and looked out the window, as they reached a set of gates. Slowly, they rolled open, and then the truck was limping inside.

"Tiffany," she heard bellowed, from the huge building they were parking beside. She turned slightly and found her brother running full barrel for the back doors. She leapt up, and hurried to the back, waiting impatiently as Steele unlatched and opened the doors.

Then arms encircled her from behind, and someone lowered her down to Preacher. She sobbed, as her brother held her tight, and thanked god she had made it back to him. She could barely breath, he was holding her so tight, but she loved it. She clung to him for what felt like hours before he finally set her down.

Tiffany looked back and found Shadow was standing beside them. She reached over and grabbed his hand, wanting the contact.

"Ah honey," you shouldn't have done that," Trike said. She was about to question him, but didn't get the chance. Her hand was pulled out of Shadow's, as Preacher shoved her behind him.

"What the fuck," Preacher shouted, as his hands balled into fists, and he charged at Shadow.

Chapter Twenty
Shadow

Shadow stood his ground as Preacher charged at him. He was a Seal, and he didn't run. He knew Preacher would be furious at him for being with his sister, and he knew if he wanted a chance with her, he needed to take Preacher's crap.

Preacher got one punch in, that rocked his head back, but when he went to throw another one, Tiffany jumped in the way. Preacher pulled his punch, at the same time Shadow hooked an arm around her waist, and pulled her behind him.

"Fuck Tiff," Preacher roared. "I could have taken your head off. Don't do that again," he ordered, as he wagged his finger at her.

Shadow watched, as she looked up at her big brother with puppy dog eyes. "You hurt him, you hurt me," she cried. Shadow saw a trickle of blood run down her lip. Preacher just stared at in in horror.

"I told you not to talk baby girl," Shadow said, in concern. He swiped his thumb over the blood and turned to Preacher.

"Can we settle this later, I need Doc to take a look at her," he sighed. "I'm not going anywhere, you can fuck me up later."

Dagger swaggered up then. "You should get back in the truck, and tie those fucking doors shut brother," he said. "Preachers gonna mess up that pretty face of yours," he helpfully said, as he kept on walking, and disappeared into the clubhouse.

Tiffany looked horrified at her brother, but most of the bikers were chuckling. Shadow just stood there, wondering if he should take the brothers advice, but with his luck, he'd fall asleep and wake up naked in the desert.

Preacher broke into his thoughts when he roared Doc's name. He was studying his sisters neck and had also just noticed her wrists and ankles. Doc's head appeared in the doorway, yelling to bring her to his room, just as Mario sauntered up.

"I'll take off then, let you get settled. I'll keep my men patrolling the streets. Any hint of The Outlaws, we'll give you a shout," he told them. "You need me, you call," he ordered, then he turned, and climbed in one of the cars. The brothers watched as he pulled out and disappeared down the road.

As they headed in, another car pulled into the parking lot. When it stopped, out stepped Tripp and Darren, the two detectives. Tripp got to the point immediately.

"Looks like a bad accident on Route 23," he said. "Car exploded and took out a couple others close by. Must have been a gas leak," he said. "You may want to stay away from that area for a while," he advised.

"Gas leak," Steele said, with a snicker.

"Yep, the emergency workers found a ton of gas around the wreckage," Tripp said. Then he pulled what was left of the two bundles of dynamite out of his suit pocket and handed them to Steele.

"Appreciated, brother," Steele said, as he took the evidence. "You ever want a change of careers, or need help with anything, you call me," he ordered.

"You never know," Tripp mumbled. "I've got eyes on all the roads in, and I'm keeping my ear to the scanners," he said. "You got us if you need us," he said. Steele nodded, and thanked him, so the detectives took off.

"Love those boys," Dagger said. "I think they like us too," he said, as a huge smile graced his face.

"Fucker," Dragon said, as he came up behind them. Then he turned to Preacher. "What do you need," he asked.

"I want men by the gate," he ordered. "Those assholes get close, I don't want to be left with my ass hanging out. Sniper, you and Raid take the roof. Those fuckers may come in hot and heavy, and you're our best chance."

"You got it," Sniper said, as he and Raid took off.

Shadow scooped up Tiffany and marched towards the clubhouse with her, not wanting to chit chat any longer. He heard stomping and turned to see Preacher right behind him.

"Why the fuck are you carrying her," he argued.

"Because she's fucking hurt and tired," he told his prez.

"After she's looked after, I'm gonna knock your head off," he promised.

Shadow entered the common room and weaved through the tables. As he passed one, Tiffany leaned down, and picked up a sandwich someone had left out. He was trying to hold in his laugh, as she leaned over his shoulder, and hurled it at her brother. It smacked him, right in the side of the head.

Chapter Twenty One
Shadow

Tiffany was placed on a bed, in a room that looked like it belonged in a clinic. Shadow stayed, but moved out of the way, as an older man approached. She moved back, not knowing him, but her brother stopped her.

"Tiff, this is our club doctor. He's a good man, I trust him," he soothed her. She nodded and forced herself to relax. The doctor smiled at her as he studied her.

"They call me Doc," he said. "I treat these hooligans when they need it, and their sweet girlfriends. I won't hurt you, but it looks like we need to clean up your wrists and ankles, and I want to take a look at your throat." She nodded, then looked to Shadow, who was leaning against the wall, and her brother, who was sitting beside her.

Doc didn't waste any time and got right down to work. He took a hold of the torn up tee shirt Shadow had used as a temporary bandage and carefully removed it. After studying her wrist, he smiled.

"It doesn't look too bad," he told her. "You've got some raw spots, but you don't need any stitches. I'll clean it, apply some ointment, and get clean wraps on it," he promised. Then he did exactly that.

The antibiotic stung, and she tried to pull her arm back, but Preacher stopped her by wrapping his arm around her waist. She saw Shadow had a pissed look too as he stepped forward. She reached a free hand out and latched on to his.

"Jesus," her brother said. "How do you expect Doc to fix your wrists, if you're holding his hand?"

She turned and glared at her brother. She knew he had a problem with her and Shadow, but she wished he'd relax.

"Baby girl," Shadow said, gaining her attention. "We kind of have an unwritten rule, that you don't mess with a brothers family. I'm not respecting my club prez by falling for his sister, you're off limits," he admitted.

She shook her head, expressing how much she didn't care. But he only smiled at her sadly, and then dropped her hand, stepping back.

"Let Doc finish. We'll figure this out later," he said. Tiffany looked down sadly and nodded. She really hoped her brother didn't pressure him to stay away from her.

Doc finished her other wrist and ankles, then moved on to her throat. He gently probed it, which hurt, and then had her open her mouth so could examine the inside.

"The throat has over fifty small muscles in it," he explained. "It doesn't take much to damage them. Your throat looks extremely raw and swollen, so I'm pretty sure that's what's happened. There's not a lot we can do for it. But for starters, you need to stop speaking for at least three weeks. The other thing I suggest, is to drink hot lemon tea with honey. That will sooth it. Can you get anything down," he asked.

Shadow answered for her. "No, but Sniper bought some Boost, and that seems to be working."

"Excellent," Doc said. "That's smart. Okay honey, that's all I can do for you," he explained as he stood up. "Promise me you'll get lots of rest."

Preacher answered for her. "I'll make sure." Then he helped her up off the bed. "She can stay in my room", he said as he glared at Shadow. Shadow just watched as her brother led her away.

She had no idea if that meant whatever they had between them was done, but it was disappointing when he didn't stop them. She dropped her head and pulled her arm from her brothers grasp. When they reached the end of the hall, and were about to turn the corner, she took a chance and looked back.

Shadow was standing in the doorway, watching her. When he caught her eyes, he placed his hand on his heart and tapped it. She finally released the breath she hadn't realized she'd been holding. He wasn't giving up, and he'd just let her know.

Chapter Twenty Two
Shadow

Shadow moved back to the common room and sat at the bar. He had no idea where to go, or what to do. Preacher was pissed, and he understood it, but he was a good man and an ex Seal, he'd never hurt the man's sister. But, with The Outlaws declaring war, now wasn't the time for this either.

Dragon moved to the seat beside him and sat down. He reached over the counter and grabbed two beers, handing him one. Shadow nodded his thanks.

"You need to let Preacher work this out," Dragon told him. "That's his little sister that got taken and hurt. You got to remember, you weren't here when we got my Ali back from that fuckers brother. My girl was a mess, and she'd been through hell. But it destroyed me to see her like that. It broke something in me. If Preacher feels half of what I feel, he won't be doing so good."

"I understand that, but I need to be there for her too, and I can't do that if the fucker won't even let me get close to her," he complained.

"Yep, I see your point too," he admitted. "I'm thinking we need to get the girls together, or at least Ali and Tiffany. Your girl's been through some of what mine has. Ali could talk to her, and I think it could help both of them. My Ali still has nightmares some times, and the odd time she just stares into space, and I lose her for a while," he explained sadly.

"Fuck brother, I'm sorry," he said.

They sat there for another fifteen minutes before Preacher stomped in from the hall. He saw them sitting at the bar, and growled, pointing at Shadow.

"You," he snarled. "Outside now." Then he stomped out the doors, and Shadow reluctantly followed. He turned when he heard footsteps and found that most of the brothers were following them. Great he thought, so this would be hashed out in public.

Preacher had stopped in the middle of the compound, close to where they had their weekend barbecues and fires, and was waiting for him. His glare said it all, this would not be a friendly chat. The brothers moved to the side, so they weren't in the way, as Shadow stopped in front of his prez.

"I sent you to retrieve my sister, not fuck with her," he roared.

"I'm not fucking with her," he shot back angrily. "I care about the girl, and I want to be with her."

"You disrespected me by doing that," he growled.

"And I'm sorry about that," Shadow admitted. "But it's not something I planned. I was drawn to her the moment I laid eyes on her. She's my one," he stated, as he stared Prez in the eye. "She makes my heart beat faster, and she gives me a purpose. I just want a chance to make her happy," he pleaded. "I can't survive without her, now that I know what it's like with her."

"So you're choosing her over the club and your brothers," Preacher said in surprise.

"Fuck," he roared. "I don't want to make that choice. Leaving her would break me," he told Preacher.

"You telling me you love her," Preacher said. "Fuck brother, it's only been a couple days."

"You find you're one, you'll know," Shadow declared.

"You hold still, you take your punishment, and I'll give you my approval," Preacher told him. "Five hits, and I'm going to make them hurt," Preacher said, as he smiled.

Shadow nodded and stood his ground. The brothers all moved to surround them. The first hit was to the jaw, and Shadow rocked back on his heels. The prez packed a hell of a punch. The second two were to the ribs, and he was sure it broke one. Another hit, and he knew he'd be sporting a black eye. The last was too his side, and with the broken rib, it doubled him over, and made it hard to breathe.

Shadow breathed in and out, to stop himself from passing out, as Preacher stepped back in front of him. Preacher raised his hand, and Shadow shook it.

"You got my blessing," his prez said. "But you hurt ever a hair on that girl's head, and I'll put a bullet in yours." Then he turned, and walked away, but he yelled over his shoulder.

"We got a war coming, get the doctor to patch you up, and get your ass ready."

Steele came over then, and thumped him on the back, sending him almost to his knees again. "You got balls brother," he said. "You need us to carry you inside," he chuckled.

Shadow stuck up his middle finger as he limped to the door. Fucker thought he was being funny, but Shadow wondered if maybe that wasn't such a bad idea after all.

Chapter Twenty Three
Tiffany

Tiffany slowly woke, unsure of where she was. As she blinked and looked around, she realized she was in her brother's room, at the compound. She had crashed last night, after seeing the doctor, and had slept like the dead. She felt better, so the sleep must have done her good. Slowly, she climbed off the bed, and headed for the attached bathroom. After cleaning up, she came back out, to stare at the door into the hall.

She was unsure about heading into the main areas of the compound by herself, but she also knew she couldn't hide in her brother's room all day. She looked down at her brother's shirt and sweats, that he had given her to wear last night, and shrugged. It was all she had, so it would have to do. She cracked the door, then peered around it.

Tiffany jumped, when a hand appeared and pushed it open completely. She took a tiny step back as a biker stepped into the doorway. He made her extremely uncomfortable, and she instantly disliked him. Glancing at his vest, she realized he was a prospect, and not a fully patched in member.

"Names Snake," he rumbled. "Preachers in the common room. He asked me to bring you to him when you woke up." Then the biker turned and walked down the hall. She followed, but at a slower pace, not wanting to get too close to him. All she could think, was that his name fit him.

When they reached the main room, Snake pointed out the table her brother was sitting at, then walked away. She actually breathed a sigh of relief once he was gone. She barely made it a foot when her brothers eyes locked on hers. He smiled, and pushed out of his seat, heading her way.

When he reached her, he grabbed her, pulling her in tight to his chest for a hug. She loved his hugs, he always felt like a massive teddy bear to her. Finally, he pulled away to study her.

"You sleep good," he asked in concern. She smiled and nodded at him. "Good, you okay," he questioned. Her smile faltered, but she nodded anyway. It would be awhile before she was okay.

Her brother frowned, but took her hand, and led her to the table he had been sitting at. She was a little unsure, but then she recognized the bikers sitting there as some of the ones that rescued her. Preacher pulled out a chair and ordered her to sit. She smiled up at him, forgetting how bossy he could be. As soon as she sat, Navaho came over, and set a mug down in front of her.

"Lemon tea, with a bit of honey darling," he explained. "It will help your throat. Start with that, then I'll bring you one of your Boost's soon." She smiled at him gratefully and mouthed a thank you. He smiled and nodded back, then moved away.

Trike, whom she remembered, then set something else down in front of her. She turned her attention to him, then looked down. He had given her a white board, with a magnetic pen attached. The board had a long string hanging from it, so she could wear it around her neck. She had to swallow a couple times, to stop the lump in her throat from getting out. The gift was extremely thoughtful.

"Thought you could use that," he said. "Doc said no talking, but I wanted you to be able to communicate. This is easier than carting around a pen and a pad of paper." Thank you she mouthed, then she leaned over and kissed his cheek.

"Trike," she heard bellowed from the other side of the room. "You better run, you little shit." She turned that way and saw Shadow slowly making his way over. When she looked back at Trike, he was rolling his eyes.

"Jesus, I'm married now," he complained. "I'm not after your woman." But he said that as he pushed his chair back and took off.

Steel was chuckling from beside her brother. "Take your time brother," he yelled at Trike's retreating back. "You could circle the room four times and the fucker would never catch you, in that state."

Tiffany turned back to look at Shadow, and cried out, as she got a good look at him. His face was bruised, he had a black eye, and he was holding his side.

Chapter Twenty Four
Shadow

Shadow observed Tiffany's face, as she pushed back her chair, grabbed something off the table, and hurried his way. He knew she'd take this hard, but the sad look on her face was killing him. She weaved through the tables, and the brothers moved out of her way.

Finally, she stopped in front of him. Her tiny hand reached up and gently smoothed over the bruise on his cheek. The warmth in the touch, made his heart beat faster. She left her hand on his cheek as she stared in horror at his black eye. Then, her hand snaked around his neck, as she pulled his head down. As soon as he was close, she stood on her tiptoes, and kissed his eye. She left her lips there for a minute, and Shadow swore he'd felt nothing better.

He still had his hand on his side, and her little head swivelled down to that next. She tried to pry off his hand, but he shook his head no.

"I'm fine baby girl," he told her soothingly, as he tried to pull her into his good side. Luckily, the Doc said Preacher had only bruised a rib, and not broken it, like he had thought. A couple days, and he'd be fine.

"Who," she mouthed to him, as she pushed out of his arms. He played dumb, and just looked at her in confusion. She angrily wrote on her board then and turned it around so he could read it. He looked down to see she had written, my brother followed by a couple question marks. He still stared at her, not admitting anything. He recognized when to keep his mouth shut.

Shadow knew Preacher was in trouble when she turned and aimed a death glare at him. She took one last sympathetic look at him, then she was moving back across the room. Shadow was trying his best to catch up to her, but his ribs were slowing him down. And, just like Trike, his baby girl was fast.

Preacher watched her warily, then stood up as soon as she reached him. He instantly raised his hands in surrender, taking a step back from her, but she matched his step. He shook his head, and then he started babbling.

"Now Tiff," he soothed. "We have rules in this club, that a brother needs to follow. You're my sister, and he disrespected me by going after you. I doled out a small punishment, then we shook hands. Alls good now, there's no reason to be angry," he tried to convince her.

She wrote fuck you on the board and held it out to Preacher. He read it, along with any of the brothers that were close, then placed his hands on his hips angrily.

"This is club business, it had to be done," he roared at her. The brothers all immediately stepped back when Preacher said that. Even they knew it was the wrong thing to say. His sister was fuming as she glared up at him.

Tiffany hauled back her foot, and Shadow watched, as she kicked her brother in the shin. Preacher bellowed, then leaned down to grab his ankle, and that's when she hauled off and kicked the other one.

"Mother fucker," he roared. He was leaned over rubbing both ankles when she balled her fist and swung. Stunned, Shadow watched, as she punched her brother right under his eye. Then the little minx wrote on the board and slammed it on the table so all the brothers could see.

There, now you match, was written on the board in capitals. All the brothers roared in laughter as Preacher turned to glare at them. That only made them laugh harder because a bruise was already forming around his eye. Tiffany had been spot on, and they would definitely match tomorrow.

Chapter Twenty Five
Tiffany

Tiffany was furious with her brother. Poor Shadow had risked his life to save hers. He had been in three gun battles since meeting her and had protected her through each one. He was kind, thoughtful, and caring. She was even more in awe of him, due to the fact that he was doing this for a stranger. He had never met her when he decided to go in on his own to save her.

After all that, Preacher had laid a beating on him. She knew there were rules and consequences in a biker club, but that was going too far. They still had The Outlaws to contend with, and Shadow's injuries meant he wasn't at one hundred percent. That wasn't what they needed right now.

Shadow tried to reason with her, explaining that he knew he shouldn't have done anything about his feelings, but he just couldn't help himself. He also told her, that the beating was the end of it, and now they could be together without any more problems. It also didn't hurt when Preacher walked through the club sprouting a black eye too. She knew she had got him good, and she couldn't be happier.

It surprised Tiffany, when that very night, Shadow moved her out of Preacher's room, and into his own. She loved curling up with him in his bed and slept so much better than she had the night before. She felt safe and at peace with him, even with his injuries.

When they woke up the next morning, they showered, then headed to the common room for breakfast. Again, Navaho brought her a tea with honey, and her Boost. Doc came by too, to check her wrists and ankles. They were healing good, but the scabs were itchy. He told her to keep on the bandages because he didn't want the scabs to get hooked and pulled off.

When she was done her Boost, Shadow took her hand and led her out the door. They headed way down the back of the property, and it surprised her to see three small cabins there. Shadow pulled her close, as he explained that when a biker found his woman, they built a cabin and moved out of the clubhouse.

Tiffany wrote on her board, asking if he wanted to do this with her. He kissed her deeply and smiled at her. Then he told her that once The Outlaws were taken care of, he'd get started right away. They walked the area and decided on a spot beside Trike's cabin. It sloped, but the views of the lake were spectacular. They sat on the spot they hoped to place the cabin and stared out at the water.

Finally, he pulled her up, and led her to one of the cabins. She was nervous when he knocked and stepped aside. The door opened, and three girls stepped out. They greeted Shadow, and he smiled as he introduced them to her.

She met Ali who was Dragon's wife, Cassie who was Steele's fiancé and Misty who was Trike's wife. Then Shadow kissed her and disappeared. Tiffany was nervous as the girls led her inside. Luckily, Shadow had already told them she couldn't talk, so that made things easier.

"You really like Shadow," Ali said happily. Tiffany nodded, as Ali continued. "He really likes you. He's quiet, and he moves around so silently, he's like a ninja," she said.

"They should have called him Ghost," Misty said giggling.

The girls then shocked Tiffany, by telling her what happened to each of them. She learned Ali had been kidnapped by The Outlaws and had been hit so hard she lost her memory. She learned Cassie's ex husband had thrown her down a well, and she learned Misty had been shot and trapped in a mine. It made her feel better knowing her situation wasn't that different from hers.

Then the girls got out ice cream, and Ali and Cassie told her they were both raped. She cried, as she told them about Bull, and ate ice cream too. Her hand was killing her by the time she was done, but she felt so much better. They spent the rest of the day laughing and telling stories.

When Shadow came by later to pick her up, she was surprised to find five hours had passed by. She hugged each of the girls goodbye and left happily after finding three new friends. On the way back to the clubhouse, she hugged Shadow, and thanked him for taking her there. She was happier than she'd been in a long time.

Chapter Twenty Six
Shadow

Four days had passed since they arrived back at the compound. Tiffany was doing well. The wounds on her wrists and ankles were healing nicely, and the bruising was fading in her neck. She had some nightmares, but Shadow was always there to sooth her, and hold her tight. Just his presence seemed to calm her.

Shadow still had bruising in his eye, but his rib was feeling a bit better. It would still be awhile before he was one hundred percent, but he was on the mend. Tiffany had visited the girl's a lot, and she seemed excited about the idea of them having a cabin of their own. As soon as they finished this shit, he would get started on it.

Things had been pretty quiet, but today The Outlaws had starting riding past the clubhouse in two's. They weren't sticking to a schedule or a certain time, but occasionally, two bikes would ride past. It looked like they were scoping the compound. Tripp and Darren had stopped them, but without weapons visible or a probable cause, the detectives couldn't hold them.

Preacher was pissed, and finally he called church to figure out what to do. Most of the brothers attended, except for Doc and Snake, who stayed at the cabin with the girls. And, Sniper and Raid, who kept watch on the roof. The gate was unmanned, but they locked it tight, and the brothers could see it from the roof. One call, was all it would take to bring out the army of bikers inside.

"How many Outlaws do you figure there are," Preacher immediately asked Shadow.

"Hammer told me the club count was thirty seven," Shadow told him.

"How many have you and the rest of the brothers taken out," he questioned.

"I took out seven at the compound," Shadow told him.

"We got six out of eight when they came at the rental," Dragon said. "The other two took off."

"And the dynamite took out another six at the roadblock," Dagger stated proudly.

"So that's nineteen dead, and eighteen fuckers left," he snarled. "That's still a lot of fire power."

"What if we take out the next two that ride past," Steele added. "They probably won't send more when they don't return, but at least that's another two of the fuckers down."

"Nah," Navaho said. "We get Sniper to shoot them, but not to kill them. We need to question them. Find out where the fuck Bull is, and what's planned." The brothers all nodded in agreement.

"I think that's a plan then," Preacher announced. "I want about eight brothers on the gate. After Sniper makes the shot I'll need one brother to open the gate, and another to stand guard," he instructed. "Then I need two brothers on each Outlaw, to drag the fuckers to the shed. The last two will get rid of the bikes," he ordered.

"I'll call Tripp, and let him know the plan, I want him and Darren clear of here. We also may need a cleanup crew on the road, if the bikes go down hard," he added.

Navaho spoke up then. "I'll make sure there's nothing left," he volunteered. Preacher nodded, knowing the brother would have the road spic and span.

"I'll head up to the roof and let Sniper and Raid know the plan," Trike said. "It's been a bit since the last Outlaws road past, so another set should pass soon."

"Right," Preacher said. "Let's leave the girls where they are for now. They don't need to know what we're doing. If things get serious, we can always move them to Mario's. His fortress may just be what we need, I don't want to be worrying about them while we take these fuckers out," he said.

The brothers nodded and got up to do Preacher's bidding. Shadow headed out with the brothers that moved towards the gate. He wanted to be one of the men dragging the assholes to the shed. Then he wanted to be one of the men that got to question them.

Chapter Twenty Seven
Shadow

Shadow hunkered down behind the gate and waited with the rest of the brothers. He wanted this shit over with. The Outlaws had kidnapped Ali, and it was their actions that started this god damned war. Shadow just wanted to find them all and end them.

They sat there for a half hour, before they finally heard the roar of pipes, as The Outlaws headed down the road towards them.

"About fucking time," Dagger complained. "My ass is asleep from sitting on the ground so long." Then he stood and headed for the gatehouse and the controls.

Shadow shook his head, then peered up to the roof of the clubhouse, to see Sniper and Raid were lining up their shots. It was decided that instead of Sniper taking both shots, they would each take out a man. Raid was almost as good as Sniper, seeing as he had the same military training, in case Sniper got taken out.

The guns fired, and the men moved. Dagger hit the button to open the gates, and the brothers filed out. Navaho had laid sawdust on the road earlier. He told the men it would absorb any oil, gas or blood spills, and make for a quick cleanup. He could literally just sweep it into the trees at the side of the road.

Two Outlaws lay on the road. One was unconscious, and it looked like he took a bullet to the shoulder. Dragon and Steele picked him up easily and carried him inside. The other biker had a bullet wound in his side and was trying to get up. Shadow walked over to him, gave him a quick kick to the head, and the man was out cold. Trike chuckled, as he moved to the other side of the biker and they hefted him up. They wanted both bikers unconscious because they didn't want any signs of a struggle.

Once they were secured inside the shed, Steele and Trike stayed with them, while him and Dragon hurried back to the road. Dagger had already pushed both the bikes inside, as they were only scratched, and Navaho had a big ass broom he was sweeping the road with. He was moving fast, but it was still gonna take a while.

"I wonder how many of those brooms we have," Dragon asked, as he watched Navaho move back and forth. Suddenly, a noise that sounded like a gas lawn mower starting up, came from right behind them. They turned, and were almost knocked off their feet, by the wind that hit them. Dagger stood there with a giant leaf blower, and it was aimed right at them.

"I bought this a while ago because it looked cool. Never got to use it though," he told them frowning. "But I think it might just come in handy right now."

Steele stared at the brother as he tried to stay on his feet. "Point that thing in another direction, before I take it from you, and shove it up your ass," he yelled over the roar of the blower. "And why the hell does it blow so hard?"

Dagger pointed it away from them, and both him and Dragon sighed in relief. "I replaced the shit motor it came with, with a Harley motor," he stated proudly.

They watched as he moved onto the road and aimed it in Navaho's direction. The broom flew out of Navaho's hands, and he turned, only to get completely covered in sawdust. Both him and Steele stood there stunned at minute, then busted out laughing. Shadow's ribs ached, but he couldn't stop.

"Mother fucker," Navaho yelled, as he battled the flying sawdust. "Turn that fucking thing off." Finally, Dagger turned the thing off, and the road was actually completely clean.

Navaho didn't care though as he spit out sawdust and wiped if from his eyes. Then he turned to Dagger, with a murderous expression on his face. Dagger dropped the tweaked blower and took off back into the compound.

"I'm gonna beat you with that fucking thing when I catch you," Navaho roared, as he took off after the brother. Both the brothers laughed again as they shut the gate and headed inside. Shadow looked up, to see Sniper and Raid were laughing as well.

Chapter Twenty Eight
Shadow

Shadow and Dragon entered the shed, and he was happy to see the brothers already had the bikers strung up in chains. It was a tight fit, as usually they only had one man in there at a time, but it would work. Raid and Sniper had stayed on the roof, and Dagger was back at the gate hiding from Navaho. The rest of the brothers were leaning against the back wall, except for Navaho and Trike who stood behind the men.

As usual, the two Outlaws wore cocky expressions, and didn't say a word. Preacher was pacing in front of them, with his hands balled in fists. He looked completely out of control, and Steele looked like he was ready to step in if the prez lost it. Finally, he stopped and stood in front of the men.

"You took my sister, and you hurt her," he sneered.

"You killed our president's brother," one biker sneered back.

"Because he took Dragon's girl, locked her up for six months, and beat the hell out of her," he roared. Shadow looked at Dragon, to see his face was a mask of pain. The brother had been lost without his girl. "You're fucking club started this shit," Preacher roared.

"And we're gonna finish it," the idiot shouted back. Preacher ignored him and turned back to the other biker.

"Where the hell is Bull holed up," he bellowed

"Somewhere you can't find him," he snorted.

Preacher started pacing again. "You know, I really was hoping you'd say that. It's been a long time since I've got my hands dirty." He walked to the tool bench and picked up a pair of bolt cutters. The brothers like their fancy knives and blowtorches, but I'm old school," he explained. "Give me a pair of bolt cutters and a hammer, and I'm good to go."

He walked towards one biker, and Shadow smirked when the man tried to back up. The chains didn't allow any movement. He reached up and grabbed the man's hand, then he placed the bolt cutters around the man's thumb.

"Anything you want to tell me," he asked. The man stared Preacher in the eye and didn't say a word. Preacher actually laughed and looked a bit crazy. "Oh goody," he said, then without a seconds hesitation, snipped the thumb off. Shadow and the brothers cringed, and the man roared. Preacher moved to the next finger and repeated the same question. Again the biker said nothing, and again Preacher snipped.

He went through the entire hand, and the man was sweating and pale, but he still wasn't talking. Preacher set down the bolt cutters and picked up the hammer. He moved to the man's knee.

"Ya gonna talk," he asked. Shadow didn't think the man could if he wanted to. "No, okey dokey," he said. Then he slammed the hammer into the man's knee. The crunch was loud, but the bikers scream was louder. Preacher then turned suddenly and drove the hammer into the side of the man's head.

"Jesus Preacher," Steele said. "What the fuck?"

"He wasn't going to talk. Besides, there's another one," he said as he pointed to the other biker. "Pass me the bolt cutters again," Preacher said to Trike.

"Don't fucking give him nothing," the biker still alive pleaded. "I'll talk, Bull's at a ranch just outside town. I'll take you there," he whined. "Oh god, please take the hammer off him," he yelled at Steele.

"Hmm," Shadow said. "A little extreme, but effective," he said.

"Yeah," Dragon said. "Preacher's always been a bit different."

"Fuck off," Preacher said. "Get the fucker down and throw him in the van. I want to check out the ranch, and make sure the fuckers there," he said.

Twenty minutes later, they were at the location. Although there were a shit ton of tire marks, the Outlaws were gone. Shadow figured, that when the two Outlaws didn't return, Bull knew something was wrong and moved the club. They were back where they started, absolutely nowhere.

Chapter Twenty Nine
Tiffany

Tiffany figured she had been at Cassie's for about five hours, when she finally heard the sound of men approaching. The girls must have heard it too because they stood and started to head for the window. Before they got close, Snake was in front, blocking their way.

"Let me check it out," he ordered. When Ali nodded, he moved to the door and peered out. Obviously liking what he saw, he threw it wide open and stepped out.

"Bout fucking time," he huffed. "I need a beer. If I never hear how hot you fuckers are, it will be too soon," he grumbled, as he walked right past the men and straight towards the clubhouse. Doc was right behind him. The bikers chuckled as they made their way inside the cabin.

"You're hot bikers have arrived," Trike yelled as he came inside. Misty squealed, and ran to him, and Ali and Cassie ran to their men.

Tiffany smiled shyly at Shadow, and he cocked a finger at her, motioning her to come to him. Her smile got bigger, then she took off running and jumped when she got close. He took a step back when she impacted, but caught her with ease.

"Hey, baby girl," he said. Then he was kissing her, and she was in heaven. When he pulled away, she mouthed hey back, then blushed when he smirked at her.

She wanted to know what had happened, but knew not to ask. Club business was club business. The bikers didn't seem overly excited, so she didn't think it was anything good.

"So you killed them all," Ali said. "It was a blood bath, and Tiffany's free." Dragon stared at her, then shook his head.

"Fuck me, I wish it were that easy," he said, as he kissed the top of Ali's head. "We're still working on it," he admitted.

"So you don't know where Bull is," she asked.

"Nope," Dragon told her.

Ali then pulled out her phone and hit a button.

"What the fuck are you doing," he questioned, but she held up her hand and shushed him. "Oh you'll pay for that later," he growled. She cocked a hip and blew him a kiss, and the other bikers laughed.

"Uncle Joe," she cried a minute later. "I miss you, when are you going to come visit me." She paused a minute, then smiled. "Well don't wait too long," she said. "Jaxon needs to speak with you," she said as she handed the phone to Dragon.

"Smart fucking woman," he laughed, as he kissed her.

Tiffany looked at Shadow, and when he looked back, she mouthed Jaxon in confusion.

"Jaxon is Dragon's real name. They've been together for a long time, so that's what she calls him. He changed it to Dragon when Bull's brother took her. For a while he thought she was dead. Dragon was the way he coped with her loss," Shadow explained. Tiffany made a sad face, trying to convey her empathy for the couple.

"Old Joe," Dragon greeted, then all the bikers and women listened, as he explained what had gone down with Tiffany. There was silence for a minute before he continued.

"I need you to ask around and see if you can find out where Bull and The Outlaws are holed up. The girls are all at risk until these fuckers are eliminated," he said. "Even your niece is a target." He paused again for a minute. "Right, later," then he hung up.

"Old Joe had word the club was heading south, but he didn't realize they were headed here. He's going to head this way and see what he can find out along the way. A couple days, and he'll be on our doorstep," Dragon told them.

Ali squealed again, thrilled with that idea. Even Shadow looked relieved. He explained that the old biker had contacts Mario didn't even know about, and that was practically unheard of.

Chapter Thirty
Shadow

The day had been a bust. After questioning the biker again, they discovered they couldn't get anything else out of him. He had told them everything he could, but he just didn't know where Bull and the Outlaws had gone. He was useless. Preacher ended up putting a bullet in his head, and Navaho and Steele took off with the body. Fifteen minutes later, the brothers were back, and they were on the way back to the compound.

Five minutes into the ride, Preacher and Steele both pulled over, when their phones went off at the same time. They both answered, then yelled furiously. The brothers all looked at each other, trying to figure out what was happening. They didn't have long to wait, before Steele was shouting orders.

"Get back on the road. The Outlaws are attacking the fucking compound," he roared. "Gates are down, and the brothers left behind can't hold them off for long."

He didn't have to say any more, as they pulled back out onto the road, and flew down it, at dangerous speeds. Shadow was scared shitless about the girls. The brothers had left them at Ali's cabin again, and only two brothers were protecting them.

No words were spoken, as the bikers roared towards the compound. The sound of the pipes was defeating, and The Outlaws would know they were coming. As soon as they got close, they could see the gates were hanging at an odd angle, and looked like someone had blown them off.

"They sacrificed their men, knowing we'd get the ranches location and head there," Preacher yelled, as they pulled through the mangled gates. Immediately, gunfire was heard all around them. The brothers parked their bikes and jumped off, pulling their guns, as they headed for the fight.

Sniper and Raid were still on the roof, and there were several dead Outlaws laying on the pavement.

"They breached the compound," Sniper yelled. "Some got past us and are inside." Steele nodded at the men, and yelled for them to stay put. All the brothers then ran into the main building.

As soon as they got through the doors, all hell broke loose. Some Outlaws were dead, and were laying on the floor, but others were alive and shooting at Snake and Dagger who were hunkered down behind the bar.

Shadow lined up a shot, and took one biker out, as Preacher took out another. The Outlaws suddenly realized they weren't alone, and turned to fire at them too. That was their mistake. As soon as they turned their backs, Snake and Dagger took them out.

They heard more gunfire from the hall, where the rooms were located, so that's the direction the brothers ran. Dragon was in the lead, and was hit by the first bullet that came their way. It caught him in the arm, but didn't slow him down. He fired three quick shots, and took the biker down.

More Outlaws appeared, popping out of the rooms, and the men opened fire. Shadow took out two himself, and he knew the other brothers took out four more. When all was quiet, the brothers searched the other rooms, making sure they got them all. Navaho appeared from the back. The brother had snuck around the building, and had entered from a window.

"What were they doing," Raid asked, as he came down the stairs leading from the roof.

"Looking for Tiffany," Shadow roared. As he ran for the door, and headed toward the cabins.

Mario must have arrived while they were inside, because him and his men were shooting at the stray Outlaws, that had managed to escape out the back door. Shadow ignored them all, as he dodged bullets and ran faster. He could hear the footsteps of his brothers, right behind him, and knew they were worried about the girls too.

The sound of bullets behind them faded away, as all Shadow could think about was his baby girl. He hoped like hell they got there in time.

Chapter Thirty One
Tiffany

Tiffany loved hanging out with the girls, but she was sick of writing everything down. She wanted to talk, even if was just choppy sentences. Her hand kept cramping, and it took too long. She was having fun though. Last time she came, Ali and Dragon's daughter was asleep, but this time Catherine was wide awake.

It thrilled Tiffany when Ali let her hold her. The girl was only a couple months old and was so tiny. She hadn't been around many babies, so she was loving this. When the tiny girl grabbed onto her finger, and smiled up at her, Tiffany fell in love. Immediately, she wondered what Shadow's baby would look like. She bet his would be even cuter if that was possible.

Suddenly, a loud boom sounded, from the direction of the clubhouse. The girls immediately stopped talking and ran to the porch. A small plume of smoke was rising into the sky.

"What the hell is that," Cassie asked fearfully.

The men had gone to take out The Outlaws, and there were only a few left to guard the clubhouse. The girls were pretty much on their own, and even though the cabins were a ways away from the clubhouse, if you looked close enough you'd see them in the distance.

Shoots rang out, and Catherine started to cry. Tiffany handed the baby over to Ali, who instantly pulled her close and started to sooth her. Tiffany had no idea what to do, she was terrified that the men had been led away on a wild goose chase.

"They've come for me," she wrote on her board.

"You three get in the cabin and lock the doors, and cover the windows," Misty ordered. "I'm going to my cabin, but I'll be back in just a minute," the girl said, before she raced away.

"Where the hell is she going," Cassie yelled.

"I don't know," Ali said, "but I think we should do as Misty suggested." She then turned and hurried back into the cabin, with Tiffany and Cassie running after her.

They hurried to the back of the house and started locking doors and windows. Luckily, the cabin wasn't huge, so it was done quickly. The girls tipped the crib up, and dragged it over to the back door, barricading it even more. Then, they used the dining room table, to block the living room window. It didn't cover it completely, but it got most of it.

The girls then tipped over the couch, and dragged it close to the living room wall, furthest from the window. They threw some blankets and pillows on the floor and got Ali and Catherine settled behind it.

A minute later, Misty came flying through the door. Her arms were filled with three shot guns. They locked the door behind her while she laid them in the floor in the middle of the room. Tiffany watched her hurry to the kitchen as she and Cassie used the coffee table to block the front door.

When Misty came back out, she was carrying several large butcher knives. She laid them down beside the rifles, then turned to the girl, with a serious expression.

"Does Dragon have any guns hidden in the cabin," she asked Ali.

"There's a hand gun in the bedroom nightstand," she said. Then she laid a now sleeping Catherine in the blanket pile and hurried off to get it. As soon as she returned, Misty barked orders.

"Ali, you stay behind the chesterfield with Catherine. That babies our priority. You use Dragon's hand gun if you need to, but only as a last resort. Cassie, you, Tiffany and myself are going to hunker down behind the coffee table. We need to catch them if they come this way. We can't let them get in the cabin. Do you know how to shoot," she asked. Both girls nodded.

Tiffany was terrified, but Preacher had taken her shooting several times. She knew after everything Cassie had been through, Steele would have shown her too. She also knew that Misty's brother was a marine sniper, so he would have taught her as well.

Ali got settled with Catherine, and the girls got comfortable behind the coffee table. They weren't worried about the back of the cabin because it faced the lake. Each girl had a rifle, and each girl looked terrified, but determined. Tiffany just prayed no one got hurt, and she hoped Shadow and the men got to them in time.

Chapter Thirty Two
Tiffany

Tiffany was the first to notice the men headed for the cabin. She slammed her hand against the coffee table, to get the other girl's attention. As soon as they looked at her, she pointed at the men that were coming their way. It was hard to tell, as they were far away, but she was pretty sure they were Outlaws. She stared hard and made out six of them.

The girls all stayed hunkered down and checked their guns. They removed the safety's and set the extra cartridges Misty had brought in front of them. They each had a knife laid close by and were prepared for anything. Ali and Catherine remained completely hidden behind the chesterfield.

As the men got closer, Tiffany recognized them. They were definitely Outlaws, and she could make out Bull in the front. They were running flat out for the cabins. Tiffany could still hear gunfire, so she knew some of The Outlaws still fought the bikers that had been left behind. The gunfire was good because it meant The Stone Knight's men were still alive and fighting.

The Outlaws were almost on them now, so Tiffany opened the small windows at the bottom, and pushed out the screen. They were just big enough, that the three girls could easily stick their barrels out, and still remain covered. As soon as they got close, the three girls fist bumped each other, then turned their attention to the men.

"Take your time, and make your shots count," Misty instructed. "Fire," she yelled, and the three girls pulled their triggers.

One man fell, but instead of getting excited, the girls remained steady, and fired again. Another man went down, but it was obvious they only wound him, when he rolled to his side, and pushed himself back to his feet.

The men immediately fired back. The window shattered, and the girls screamed and covered their heads, as glass rained down on them. They looked at each other, and noticed they had had small scratches, but none of them were seriously hurt. They turned back to the window and continued to fire.

They ended up hitting two more men, and when the men fell, they didn't get back up again. The sound of the gunshots had woken up Catherine, and Ali was trying to calm the screaming baby. Bullets still flew, and some were coming right threw the drywall.

The girls were still firing and hurrying to reload in between shots. The Outlaws had taken cover behind some trees and were firing at them non stop.

Suddenly Cassie screamed, and Tiffany turned to her, horrified to see a bullet had torn through her arm. Misty ripped off her sweater and wrapped it around the girl's arm. Tiffany continued to fire as more bullets tore through the walls. The men were better shots, and Tiffany was terrified that this would end bad.

Suddenly, the firing stopped, and she cringed, when she heard Bull's voice.

"Tiffany, if you care about those girls, and that fucking baby I hear screaming, you'll get your god damned ass out here. You've got one minute until we open fire, and kill the fucking lot of you," he roared.

Tiffany looked at Cassie, who was crying and holding her arm, then to Misty who was holding onto Cassie. Finally, she looked to Ali, who was peaking over the couch, while trying to sooth Catherine.

"I have to go," she mouthed.

"No you don't," Cassie said, as she shook her head. "I can still shoot. We can do this," she pleaded.

"Thirty seconds," Bull yelled. "You ready for a blood bath," he taunted.

Tiffany watched the girls a second longer, then made her decision. She stood and hurried to the door, then she pushed the table out of the way.

"I'm sorry," she mouthed. Then she threw open the door and ran straight towards Bull. She knew she probably won't make it through this, but the other girls would. Just before she reached him, she raised her rifle and fired off two quick shots. Both hit the two Outlaws that were with Bull, but she had been so close, her shots would have had to have been horrible, to have missed.

She turned the gun on Bull, but the man moved quickly, and knocked it out of her hand. A second later she had no time to react, as his fist flew at her face, and she was knocked unconscious.

Chapter Thirty Three
Shadow

Shadow booted it across the field. His only focus was getting to the cabin, and Tiffany. He knew his brothers were right behind him; they sounded like a herd of elephants, as their boots crushed the ground. It was a good ten-minute hike, but Shadow made it in four. As soon as he got close, he could see the bodies riddled across the grass. Dragon bellowed and immediately yelled Ali's name.

As they got closer, they noticed the bodies weren't their women, but the bodies of The Outlaws.

"We need to see if any of the assholes are still alive," Steele said, as his eyes darted between the bodies and the cabin.

"Go," Navaho ordered. "Me, Sniper and Raid got this. See to your women. Make sure they're okay."

Steele nodded, and the men were off again. They pounded up the cabin steps and literally crashed through the door as a unit. Shadow was shocked, by the sight that greeted him. Bullets had torn through the side of the cabin and were embedded in the walls of the living room. Furniture was overturned and scattered throughout the room, and guns, knives and ammunition, lay on the floor. It looked like a war had been fought.

The girls were huddled in the middle of the floor, crying and clinging to each other. When they noticed the bikers, they sobbed even louder. Trike moved to Misty, and picked her up, dragging her to his chest tightly. It looked like the brother was never gonna let her go. Dragon engulfed both Ali and his baby girl in his arms, cradling them against his chest and rocking back and forth.

Steele saw the blood on Cassie's arm and flipped. He threw a table out of the way, and roared, as he headed for her.

"I'm okay," she whispered to the broken biker. "The bullet went through, it's not that bad," she tried to sooth him.

Those words only caused Steele to lose it even more. He crushed her in his arms as he pulled out his phone. A minute later he was talking.

"Need you at the clubhouse now," he roared. "I don't fucking care, walk out if you have too. The Outlaws were here, and Cassie was shot in the arm. There may be more injuries, I just don't know." Steele paused a minute before speaking again. "Right," he said then hung up. He looked at the brothers. "Doc was on shift, but he's bugging out. He'll be here in fifteen."

"Where's Tiffany," Shadow asked the girls. He had a bad feeling, and he was starting to sweat.

"She gave herself up," Cassie cried.

"We begged her not too," Misty said. "But, Cassie was shot, and the biker threatened to kill us all. We took out three, but there were three left when she went out.

She killed two more before the biker took her gun and knocked her out," Misty told the brothers.

"Tiffany saved us," Ali added. "She didn't want us hurt further. She was scared to death for us and Catherine," she said.

Both Shadow and Preacher roared in anguish. Bull now had Tiffany, and they knew he meant to kill her.

"You did good girls," Steele told them. "I'm so proud of you. You defended yourselves, and you killed five men. But, this never should have happened. You shouldn't have been left on your own," he said brokenly.

"Tiffany," Cassie cried. "You need to go after Tiffany. Bull has about a ten minute head start."

Steele looked down at his woman, and Shadow knew the brother was torn. He wanted to go with them, but he didn't want to leave her.

"You stay with the girls," Preacher ordered. "You get her fixed up, and you get the clubhouse locked down. Raid, Dagger, Sniper and Snake can help you. There's just Bull left, so we don't need you. Mario should still be here, tell him to be on standby in case I need him."

Then Shadow, Preacher, Dragon and Trike left the cabin, and headed for the trees.

"Navaho," Preacher called, before they got too far. "Any alive." Navaho only shook his head. "Need your tracking skills brother. Bull took Tiffany, and you gotta find them."

The brother said not a word. Just stood and headed for the trees. If anyone could find her, he could.

Chapter Thirty Four
Shadow

Shadow, and the brothers followed closely behind Navaho. The brother moved quickly, but his eyes never left the ground. But, even Shadow could have followed most of the trail. Bull wasn't trying to hide his tracks, he was just trying to get away, as fast as he could. Branches were snapped off, and the ground was trampled.

They kept at it for fifteen minutes until they came out at the road. Obvious tire tracks were there, but there was no sign of either him or Tiffany. Navaho shook his head in defeat.

"Sorry brothers," he said to them all. "I can't track a car. But, it may have been one of the SUV's. The wheel marks look further apart, and the car sat heavier," he explained.

"Fuck," Shadow roared. "He's gonna fucking kill her. We don't have time for this."

"I feel the same as you," Preacher said. "But we need to get back to the clubhouse. We need our bikes, and we need help," he ordered.

"God dammit," Shadow said in agitation. Then, he turned and jogged down the road, in the direction of the compound. Again, the brothers were right behind him. It took them only ten minutes to get there.

The amount of damage that had been done floored Shadow. The gates had literally been blown off their hinges. They were mangled, twisted pieces of metal. When he moved through, all he saw was bodies. It was obvious, the brothers and Mario and his men, had dragged out the dead Outlaws and piled them up outside.

Mario, and his right-hand man Trent, moved to them as soon as they saw them.

"The girls," Mario asked.

"Good," Preacher explained. "Barricaded themselves in the cabin and took out five men with a couple rifles. Cassie took a bullet to the arm, but she'll be okay."

"Tiffany," Mario asked next.

"Gone," Shadow answered, before Preacher could. "Bull seems to be the only Outlaw left alive. He lured her out of the cabin, then took off."

"Mother fucker," Mario swore. "Any idea where he took her."

"No," Preacher said. "But we don't have a lot of time. He wants blood for blood, so he's gonna kill her."

"Shit," Mario said, just as a car pulled into the compound. Tripp and Darren stepped out.

"What the hell happened," Tripp asked angrily.

"Outlaws stormed the castle and took the princess," Dagger said, as he made his way towards them. "What the fuck are we gonna do about it," he asked. Tripp just blinked at the brother.

"You pass a black SUV on your way here," Shadow asked Tripp.

"No, but there was an accident in town, so we came from that direction," Tripp explained.

"So that means he took her out of town," Dagger said.

"Right, but that means he could have her anywhere," Mario said. "I'll get my men to split up and look," he said, as he gave instructions to Nick. The man then headed off, to relay what he had been told.

Finally, Doc pulled into the parking lot. He didn't waste any time jumping out and hurrying over to them.

"Where's Cassie," he asked.

"Right fucking here," Steele roared, as he walked up holding Cassie in his arms. The girls were all behind him, along with Sniper, who had a sleeping Catherine in his arms.

"Didn't want to leave them at the cabin. They killed five men, they can deal with the carnage. Besides, it's better if we stick together, and Doc may have other men he needs to attend," Steele growled. Dragon then moved forward and took his daughter from Sniper.

"You taught your sister well," Ali told Sniper. "She had us all battle ready in minutes. Probably saved our lives," she added. Sniper moved to Misty and wrapped her in his arms.

"We need to teach the girls to use dynamite," Dagger said. "It's quicker and more effective."

"No dynamite," everyone yelled at once. Dagger just looked away and headed back in the direction he came.

"Let's make a plan," Preacher ordered. Then all the brothers, Mario and the detectives hunkered down, and got to work.

Chapter Thirty Five
Tiffany

Tiffany was groggy and did not understand why. Her head hurt, and her mouth was parched. She opened her eyes slowly, unsure of whether or not she actually wanted to. Horrified, she discovered she was hanging from chains, and dangling a foot above the ground. The chains were attached to her wrists, and it pulled her arms high above her head. Someone dressed her in a tiny, white silk nighty.

Suddenly, like a flood, everything came back to her. She remembered Misty getting the guns, and the girls shooting at The Outlaws. She also remembered giving herself up to save them. Cassie had been shot, and she was terrified the bikers would keep firing, until they were all dead. She also remembered shooting Bull's two club members.

That meant that Bull was around here somewhere. She craned her neck, trying to see him, but he wasn't there. She then tried to figure out where she was. It appeared to be a warehouse of some sort, but it was completely empty. The chains were attached to a beam high in the ceiling. There were windows, but they were small, and high up.

The warehouse was pretty dark inside, and shadows covered the entire thing. If the chains didn't terrify her, the creepy shadow's would. She tried twisting and spinning, desperate to free herself. But it was no use, the chains were tight, and they didn't even move. Blood ran down her wrists, and she instantly stopped.

She knew she was in serious trouble, and she didn't think she could do anything about it. She took a quick survey of her body. Nothing hurt, and she couldn't see any damage. She was in a nighty, with nothing under it, but she knew from experience that Bull hadn't raped her.

She had no idea what his plan for her was. He wanted her dead; he had said that repeatedly, but from the state she was in, she wondered how soon that would happen. Bull was crazy, so she didn't even want to try to figure out what he was thinking.

Her thoughts then moved to her brother and Shadow. It would devastate her brother. Her death would break him. She knew he would blame himself, and she hoped his club helped him. She knew they were close like family, they'd get him through this.

Tiffany had no idea how Shadow would react. Their relationship was so new that she didn't want to guess his feelings. He had tapped his chest over his heart a couple times, but he hadn't actually said the words. She loved him, but she was too afraid to tell him. Plus, she really wanted to say the words, and not write them down.

She prayed then that Shadow or Preacher would find her in time. The way things looked, it was unlikely, but the other girls had been in bad situations, and their men had come through. She knew she needed to have faith, but right now that was hard. Whatever Bull had planned, it was going to bad, and she didn't know how long she would be able to hold on.

Suddenly, she remembered Shadow's dog tags. They had been around her neck when she had been taken, but they were nowhere to be seen now. She cried at the loss of them. She knew they were important to him, but they meant the world to her. They brought her comfort, and she loved to hold them. She hoped Bull hadn't destroyed them.

She heard a noise to the right of her and craned her neck trying to see. Suddenly, a door opened, and she watched as Bull prowled in. He had a huge smile on his face as he looked at her. She also noticed he had a bag slung over his shoulder, but she had no idea what was in it.

"Ah my beauty, it's about time you woke up. I was beginning to think I hit you too hard." He dropped the bag on the floor, about a foot from her. "It's time to play," he said happily.

Chapter Thirty Six
Shadow

Shadow was loosing it. Mario's men had checked in, to let them know there was no sign of Bull. Tripp and Darren couldn't find anything, and the brothers that were out looking, came back empty handed as well. Tiffany had been gone two hours now, and it wasn't looking good.

Preacher had broken four of the tables in the common room before the brothers had taken him down. The prez was now sitting at the bar, nursing a whiskey, and talking quietly with Steele. He was pale, and still looked furious, but he was calmer.

Shadow wanted to trash the room too, but his training kept him calmer. He was keeping himself together until he got a hold of Bull. When that fucker was found, Shadow was taking him out.

Steele's cell rang, and he answered it on the second ring. He listened for a minute, then hung up.

"Dagger said there's a young boy at the gate, and he's asking for Preacher and Shadow," he told the brothers. That got all the brothers moving, they rose and headed for the gate as a unit. When they reached it, sure enough there was a kid, waiting on a bike. He looked a little freaked when all the brothers headed for him. Shadow looked at Preacher as they stopped in front of the kid.

"Some guy paid me fifty bucks to give you this," the boy said, as he handed them a plastic grocery bag.

Preacher took the bag, opened it to look inside, then roared in obvious pain. Shadow grabbed the bag off him and looked inside as well. His heart stopped, when he saw the clothes she had been wearing, folded neatly in the bottom. He reached in and grasped the dog tags that had been placed on top and brought them out. He fisted them against his heart for a minute, then put them back around his neck.

"She's dead," Preacher roared. "Fucker killed my baby sister. This is his way of letting us know." Then the prez fell to his knees and dropped his head. He was breaking, and there was nothing they could do.

Shadow immediately turned to the kid. "Where were you, when the man gave you this stuff," he questioned. His brothers closed in, wanting to hear the kids answer as well.

"I was at the gas station, putting air in my tires. He drove up beside me in a black rig, stuck his head out the window, and asked if I wanted to make some quick cash. He handed me the bag, some cash, and headed out of town," the boy explained.

"So he could be anywhere," Shadow said. "That doesn't help."

Mario stepped forward then. "She could still be alive. If she was dead, he most likely would have sent a stronger message. Besides, he wants you to suffer, you'll know when he does the deed. The fuckers messing with you," he told them.

"Makes sense," Shadow said. "The pricks crazy, he's gonna drag it out, and he's gonna want you to see the body."

Preacher lifted his head and looked at them hopefully. "She's still alive," he stated.

"She's still alive," Shadow said back.

Then Preacher's phone rang. He pulled it out and answered it right away.

"Preacher," he said. Then he paused a few minutes and listened intently. The man suddenly climbed to his feet, and the look on his face changed from one of pain, to one of almost glee. "I owe you," he said, then he hit a button, and shoved the phone in his pocket.

"That was Old Joe," Preacher told the brothers. "He got word that Bull's holed up at the old coal warehouse, just outside of town. Get the fuck on your Harley's, or I'm leaving without you," he said, as he charged to his bike and climbed on.

Shadow reached his next, followed by the entire club. The roar of the Harley's starting up was defeating. They pulled out of the compound, and three cars pulled out behind them. Shadow knew Mario wouldn't be missing this. He pushed his bike as fast as it would go, praying they got there in time.

Chapter Thirty Seven
Tiffany

Tiffany watched in horror, as Bull squatted on the ground, and emptied his bag. The first thing he pulled out, was a wicked looking knife, it had a short handle and a long curved blade. The second thing to come out, was a wooden baseball bat. The next thing to come out, scared her the most. It looked like a car battery, with jumper cables attached to it. The last item, was a deep, square pail.

She watched, as he shook his head for a minute, then turned and walked out the door he had entered. It was only a minute later, that he came back, carrying a large jug of water. He set it on the floor, next to the pail.

"You know," he said, as he picked the knife back up. "I hated my fucking brother. Guy was a dick. Didn't give a shit about me. Didn't really give a shit about anyone," he told her. "I actually couldn't give a fuck he's dead. But, he was my brother. It's expected that I get revenge. Kind of an honour thing," he said, as he moved to stand directly in front of her.

"You have to die," he told her. "A life for a life. Preacher killed my brother, so I have to kill you." He twirled the knife in his hand, and Tiffany's eyes shot to it. "I wanted to make you mine. You're so fucking beautiful. Pure innocence, it's why I wanted you in white. I'm sorry Beauty, but this is gonna hurt."

Bull's arm suddenly shot out, and he brought the knife up. He dragged it along her chest, just above her breasts, slicing a deep line from one side to the other. Tiffany was in agony, she'd never felt pain like that before. Tears streamed down her face, and she tasted blood, as she bit the inside of her mouth. She refused to scream, knowing if she did, there was a good chance she'd never be able to talk again. Bull stared at her chest as the blood dripped down onto the white nighty.

"Isn't that a sight," he said. "The blood stands out so well against the white. It's mesmerizing," he said. "I could stare at it forever."

Tiffany was getting light headed, and she was beginning to sweat. The pain wasn't easing, if anything, it got more intense. Bull turned and set down the knife, her blood dripping from the blade. He then picked up the baseball bat and turned back to her.

"For a tiny thing, you have stunning legs. Their long, their trim, and they belong on a cover model. I adore your fucking legs," he told her.

Then he took the bat and swung, catching her on the right knee. She heard the crack and felt the bones break. Again, she didn't cry out, but the pain left her fighting for consciousness. He swung again, and caught the same leg, but this time the bat hit below her knee. A bone actually snapped so bad, it broke through the skin.

Tiffany's head fell to her chest, and she saw black spots, as they danced in front of her eyes. She didn't see him set down the bat, but she heard the think it made, as it hit the ground. She blinked to try to clear her vision, wondering if that was even a good idea.

Bull was now filling up the pail, from the jug of water he held. It took a minute, and then he threw the jug across the floor. He bent low, and grabbed the sides of the pail, dragging it over to her. When he had it placed directly under her, he lifted her feet, and set them inside the pail. She shivered, as the cold water hit her toes.

He then moved to the battery and turned it on. She watched in horror as he cranked the dial as high as it would go. Then he picked up the booster cables and turned to face her once more.

"Time to die Beauty," he said, as he headed for her.

Chapter Thirty Eight
Shadow

When they got close to the warehouse, the entire club pulled over. They had no intention of alerting Bull to the fact they were coming for him. If he knew they were close, he'd kill Tiffany on the spot. Shadow shut off the Harley, and flipped the kickstand down, then climbed off and took off in the direction of the warehouse.

He heard the pounding of a shit ton of boots behind him, but he pushed himself harder, and reached the warehouse first. There were windows high up, but no other way to see in. There was a door, but they didn't want to use it, afraid Bull would see them, and kill her.

Shadow surveyed the outside walls, and found a drainpipe, that would get him to the ledge where the windows were. He ran for it, and grabbed on, climbing at an accelerated pace. He heard a noise below him, and looked down, to see Preacher and Steele climbing up as well. They were proceeding at a much slower pace, not having his skills.

He reached the top quickly and climbed onto the ledge. In seconds, he was standing in front of a window, and peering inside. It was dark, so it took him a minute for his eyes to adjust. When they did, he stared in horror at the sight that greeted him.

Tiffany was hanging from chains. She was wearing a white silk nighty soaked in blood. Shadow had no idea if his baby girl was alive or dead. As he watched, Bull hit the girl's leg with a baseball bat. She didn't scream, and Shadow almost did it for her. His heart broke watching her. When Bull moved away, Shadow saw the bone now sticking out of her leg. It was then that Preacher and Steele reached him.

"Jesus," Steele whispered. "We need in there now." They watched as Bull put down the bat and reached for the jug of water. Shadow saw the booster cables on the table and knew what was about to happen.

"Give me two minutes," he ordered. "Then I want every mother fucker inside that warehouse. Break through the god damned walls if you have to."

"What are you gonna do," Preacher asked.

"Get Tiffany the fuck away from him. Now move," he shouted.

He turned and sprinted for the far side of the ledge he was on. When he reached the window, he climbed inside, and headed for the beam he had picked out a minute ago. He crawled along it, as quickly as he deemed safe, and stopped when he was directly over top of his girl. Bull had her feet in the water, and the cables in his hand. He could tell by the cracking sound they made that Bull had the battery cranked.

It took everything he had to stay still and not shoot the fucker. He would have, but Bull was too close to Tiffany. If he dropped the cables, there was a chance he could hit her with them.

Suddenly, the time he waited for arrived. A fucking car, driven by none other than Mario, drove through the wall behind Bull. Bull jumped about eight feet in fright, just missing Tiffany with the cables. Shadow breathed a sigh of relief, when the fucker turned to face the army, that came flooding through the opening.

As soon as Bull was facing away, Shadow grabbed the chains and pulled, giving it everything he had. His girl was tiny, but the chains weighed a ton. His muscles strained, as he hauled her up higher, out of Bull's reach. Suddenly, her head lifted, and she looked up at him. When they locked eyes, a small smile broke through. Shadow had no idea how she could smile, with the shape she was in, but it gave him hope. His baby girl was the strongest person he knew.

Chapter Thirty Nine
Tiffany

Tiffany was practically frozen with terror when Bull picked up the booster cables and headed for her. She could barely keep her head up and was close to passing out. Her mind was fuzzy, and she was finding it hard to focus. She knew the end had come, Bull wasn't playing anymore, he was going to kill her.

The cables were too close. She could actually feel the sparks as they hit her skin. She closed her eyes, desperate to hide from his crazed stare. She pictured Shadow in her head and cried for the time they wouldn't get. Tiffany thought of Preacher next, and her heart ached for her brother. They were close, and she knew he would have let her stay with the club. He gave Shadow his blessing, and he had let them be together.

Suddenly, a loud crash sounded from behind Bull. Tiffany snapped her eyes open, to see a car had smashed through the wall. As soon as it was all the way through, a ton of bikers came rushing in behind it. Preacher was in the lead, and all the bikers had their guns out.

Tiffany felt her body lifting and had trouble trying to figure out what was going on. Bull had his back to her, and was staring at the bikers, as she rose higher into the air. Mustering what strength she had left, she raised her head, and looked up.

Shadow had somehow gotten above her, and he was pulling her up. His muscles strained, and his face was set in lines of pain, but still he pulled. When she caught his eyes, she tried to smile, but she had no idea how successful she was. He didn't smile back, but he grunted and pulled harder. She was halfway up now, and out of Bull's reach. All she could do was cry in relief. Bull was now shouting threats at the bikers.

"Come any closer, and I'll fucking kill her," he yelled. She looked back down and watched as her brother smirked at him.

"You go right ahead," Preacher laughed.

When Bull turned around, and discovered she was gone, he roared in fury. Then he looked up and roared again. He tried to reach her foot with the cables, but she was too high. He only succeeded in kicking the pail over and covering the floor in water.

The bikers converged on him as a unit then, and they ripped the cables out of his hand. They tackled him to the ground, and punches and kicks were rained down on the man.

Finally, Preacher growled at the bikers to move Bull out of the way. When he was clear, Preacher looked up at Shadow, and ordered him to lower her to the ground. Slowly, she started to descend. When she was down as far as the chains would allow, Preacher was there.

"Fuck Tiff," he said, when she looked at him. He had tears in his eyes, and she honestly couldn't remember ever seeing him cry before. She couldn't stop crying herself, and she couldn't talk, so she couldn't say anything to help him.

"I'm going to unhook the chain, and lower her the rest of the way," Shadow shouted. "Fucking catch her."

Preacher glared up at Shadow, then moved into position. It jostled her a bit, as they unhooked the chain, then she was in Preachers arms.

"Move to the right," Shadow ordered. "I'm going to throw the chain down, so you can get it off her. Someone hold the god damned thing, so it doesn't pull at her arms when I do."

Steele rushed forward and grabbed the chain just above her wrists, making sure he would take the jolt, and not her. Then Shadow threw the chain, and she didn't feel a thing. More bikers converged on her as they unwrapped the chains from her arms. She looked up, trying to see Shadow, but he was gone.

The pain was almost too much to bear now, and she knew she was going to pass out. Suddenly, Shadow appeared beside her. She had no idea how he got down so fast, but she didn't care.

"Baby girl," he said sadly, as he looked her over.

"I love you," she whispered, then she passed out.

Chapter Forty
Shadow

When Tiffany passed out, Shadow's heart stopped again. He had no idea how much more he could take. Doc immediately pushed through the men and rushed to his side. He went straight for her neck, to check her pulse.

"Her pulse is weak, but steady," he told them. "We need to stop the bleeding from her chest. I can't do anything about her leg, we've just got to leave it for now."

Raid quickly removed his vest, and whipped his shirt over his head, handing it to Doc. "Use this", he ordered. Doc placed it gently across the wound, applying pressure. Tiffany woke for a minute and blinked up at Preacher.

"Shadow," she whispered.

"You can't be talking," Shadow told her, as Preacher passed her over to him. He cradled her close as Doc kept the pressure on.

"We need to get her to the hospital," Doc instructed.

Suddenly, Bull woke, and started struggling. Preacher turned and kicked the biker in the head, instantly knocking him out again. "Get this fucker out of my sight. I want him in the shed and strung up. I'm heading to the hospital, but I'll be back later."

Mario joined them next. "My car's right there," he said, as he pointed to the middle of the warehouse. The brothers chuckled as they looked at it.

"You sure know how to make an entrance," Shadow told him, as they headed for it.

"I'm all about the show," he smirked. Then he opened the back door, and Shadow carefully climbed inside with Tiffany. Next Doc climbed in as Preacher climbed in the front with Mario.

As they backed out, Shadow watched the men drag Bull outside. When he turned, Dagger was racing after them. Mario stopped and rolled down his window.

"Can I blow the warehouse," he panted. "You're gonna fuck up Bull, so you definitely don't want any evidence left behind." He looked way too giddy as he waited for Preachers response.

"Yep," Preacher finally sighed. "But give me a fucking minute to warn Tripp. And get me the god damned booster cables and battery. I want them in the shed waiting for me," he instructed.

Dagger nodded and took off, yelling for Trike, his ever willing sidekick. Shadow watched as they grabbed sticks of dynamite from the crazy fuckers Harley and stacked them in a pile. Then Trike raced in and got the battery and cables. Next, the brothers bellowed for everyone to clear the area. As bikes were moved, and men backed away, Preacher made the call.

"Tripp brother, giving you the heads up that the old steel warehouse at the edge of town is gonna go kaboom." He paused a minute. "Rig a story up," another pause. "I don't fucking care, it's where Bull kept Tiffany." he paused again. "She's hurt bad, we're headed to the hospital now. Thanks brother, appreciated," he finished.

"Tripp will come up with something. Man's gonna get a fucking great Christmas present," Preacher said. Then he turned to Dagger and gave him the thumbs up.

Dagger grinned like the fool he was, then picked up a stick of dynamite, and passed it to Trike. He got another for himself, then the brothers lit them. They both threw them at the same time. The explosion was incredible, and the roof caved in. Debris fell in every direction.

All the brothers present, along with Mario's men, whooped and hollered. Mario shook his head and then backed up. They left the warehouse to the sounds of more explosions. Dagger was in his element now, and when he was done, there'd be nothing left.

When Shadow looked down at Tiffany, it was to find her out again. He really wanted to put the dog tags back around her neck, but he didn't want them to be in Doc's way. He decided to keep them around his neck until Doc was finished. But they would be back around her, where they belonged, soon enough. And they were never coming off again.

Chapter Forty One
Shadow

Tiffany never regained consciousness, the whole way to the hospital. Shadow and Preacher were scared shitless, seeing her injuries were so bad. Shadow tried not to think the worst, as he held her small body against his, but it was hard. The blood that covered her was hard to ignore.

When they arrived at the hospital, Mario bumped up over the curb, and drove right up to the door. Security came running out, yelling that they couldn't park there, but Doc climbed out of the car and quickly shut them down. Once they were all safely inside, Mario backed up and went to park it.

Doc raced them through the ER and took them right up to the floor surgeries were performed on. He immediately got Tiffany onto a gurney and had a couple nurses get her ready for surgery. He pushed the brothers into a waiting room, and left them there to wash up, and get into his scrubs. He assured them that her injuries weren't life threatening, but that time was of the essence.

Doc was gone for four hours, and during that time, the waiting room had filled up. Almost all the bikers had joined them, along with Mario and Trent, and Tripp. They sat silently and waited, offering their support. Bull was chained up in the shed, and Navaho and Snake had stayed behind to keep their eye on him.

Finally, an extremely tired Doc stepped into the waiting room. He headed directly for Shadow and Preacher. He ducked his head for a minute, collecting his thoughts, then raised it and sighed.

"The wounds on Tiffany's wrists weren't that bad. They've been cleaned and wrapped. The slice across her chest was deep, but I was able to stitch it easily. She may end up with a nasty scar, but I'll give her the same cream I gave the other girls, and it should help with that", he explained. Then he took in a deep breath and continued.

"Her leg was a fucking mess. Several bones in her knee were broken, and of course you saw the bone sticking out of her lower leg. I had to use several pins to repair her knee, and I've reset the bone in her leg. I've put her leg in a large splint, and I want her in a wheelchair for at least four weeks. She puts the slightest weight on that leg, and the pins will move, causing permanent damage. She's going to have a lot of therapy in the future," he told them.

"Fuck," Preacher roared as he paced the room. "Will she walk," he asked. It was something Shadow wanted to ask, but had been afraid to.

"She should be able to, but it will all depend on her recovery. I want to warn you both, there's a good chance she'll have a significant limp, and she may always have to wear a brace," he admitted.

"I want to see her," both men said at once. Doc immediately nodded and led the way. "She's sedated, and won't wake until morning, and I want to keep her for at least three days. I'd usually keep her longer, but I'll be at the clubhouse with her, so she can be monitored from there."

"Appreciated," Preacher told him. Then they were pushing the door open and heading into her room.

His poor baby girl looked so small lying in the bed. She was pale and had an IV hooked up to her arm. The blankets were pulled up to her chin, so they couldn't see her injuries, but where her right leg was, the blankets were noticeably higher. It was obvious she had a splint of some sort on it.

Preacher reached her first and kissed her on the forehead. He had tears in his eyes.

"I'm gonna let you stay with her tonight. She'll be asleep anyway. I want to spent a bit of time with Bull." He raised his hand when Shadow went to argue. "You have to be here if she wakes up. Plus, I plan on keeping Bull alive for several days. I want his death to last awhile and to be extremely painfully. I'll work him some tonight, and then I'll relive you in the morning, and you can have your fun." Shadow just looked at Preacher.

"When Tiff gets to leave, we'll take her to the compound, and when she's settled, we'll finish Bull together. Agreed," Preacher asked, as he held out his hand.

"Agreed," Shadow said, as he shook it. Their pact was made, and Shadow smirked at the thought of what they had planned for the biker.

Chapter Forty Two
Tiffany

Tiffany woke up groggily. She knew instantly she was safe. She could smell and feel Shadow at her back. It relaxed her immediately. He must have felt her move slightly because his arms tightened. She wasn't in any pain, but she remembered being hurt badly, and knew there were some things she would have to deal with.

"How you doing baby girl," Shadow asked quietly, as he propped himself up on his elbow to look down at her.

Tiffany smiled up at him and brushed her hand lightly across his cheek. "I'm okay," she whispered back.

Then she realized that her throat didn't hurt when she talked, and it hadn't when she talked yesterday either. She frowned and moved her hand from his cheek to her neck.

"Doc checked your throat and told me it looks one hundred percent better. You can't go making any long speeches, but you should be good to go," he told her.

"I love you," Tiffany instantly told him again.

He grinned down at her and instantly responded. "I love you too baby girl. You've held my heart for a while now, I just didn't know if you felt the same way. I want you to be mine forever," he told her.

She watched, as Shadow pulled off his dog tags, and placed them back around her neck. Tears ran down her cheeks as she raised her hand and gripped them tight.

"I thought Bull got rid of these," she cried. "When I woke up in the warehouse, they were gone." Shadow growled above her.

"Bull won't be around much longer, and where he is, is somewhere he can't get to you from. You're safe baby girl," he told her. "Now you let me know if my tags hurt your chest," he ordered.

"They're perfect," she told him. "And I'm not worried about Bull. I trust you completely. You got to me in time, and you saved my life."

"You scared the ever loving fuck out of me," he admitted. "I know why you gave yourself up, but promise me you won't do anything like that ever again."

"Cassie," she cried, but she didn't get any further before he was shushing her.

"The girls fine, although Steele's treating her like she broke her fucking arm," he chuckled. "He's driving her up the wall I hear."

"How bad is my leg," she asked. Shadow leaned over and kissed her on the head.

"It's bad," he told her. "You'll be in a wheelchair for a while, then you'll be looking at a shit load of physical therapy. It looks like you may always need to wear a brace, and I'm afraid you'll have a limp," he regretfully told her.

"It's okay," she told him. "Bull will be in the past, and we can start our life together. I'm a fast healer," she said, as she pointed to her throat. "I'll work hard, and get through this," she told him.

"Jesus, you amaze me," he told her. He was about to say more, but the door smashed against the wall as her brother charged into the room.

"Timothy," she cried happily when she saw him. She heard tons of laughter, as Trike, Dragon and Dagger followed him inside.

"Timothy," Dagger sputtered. "That's your name. You don't look like a Timothy," he howled, as he slapped his knee.

Preacher turned to glare at his brother as he took a step towards him. "I'll end you here, you little fucker," he growled. "You ever say that name again, I'll put a bullet in your fucking head."

Dagger immediately paled. "Right," he said quickly. "I'll never usher the name Timothy again," he told them, then he started laughing again as he fled from the room.

"Fucker knows how to get on a brothers nerve," he complained. Then he was across the room and engulfing Tiffany in his arms. She hugged him back just as tight, ignoring the pull in her chest.

"Love you big brother," she told him.

"Love you too Tiff," he growled. "Welcome to the Knights."

Chapter Forty Three
Shadow

Shadow hated to leave Tiffany in the hospital, but she was with her brother, and he was making her laugh. He was amazed at how strong she was. Even after everything that Bull had done to her, she was shrugging it off, and trying to get on with her life. She was an amazing addition to the women of the Knight's.

Shadow kissed her passionately, told her to call him for anything, then left. The smile that had been on his face only moments before, was now replaced with a look of cold hard fury. Preacher hadn't said a word about what he had done to Bull, only gave him a nod to indicate it was his turn. Shadow pushed through the doors and stopped when he saw his Harley parked right at the door. His brothers were looking out for him.

Shadow pushed his bike hard, on the way back to the compound. He was almost giddy about getting his turn in the shed. He parked close to the door of the main building and stomped over to the shed. Snake greeted him at the door, and pushed it open, allowing him entrance.

Shadow waited for a minute as his eyes adjusted to the dimmer light. When he could see clearly, he couldn't help but smile at the sight that greeted him. Bull was strung up by the chains as he expected. It looked like his right knee had been shattered, and he knew it was worse than what Tiffany's had been. Preacher had also carved the words ass, across the fuckers chest.

When he looked around, it surprised him to see Sniper, Raid and Navaho watching him. They nodded in greeting, but didn't say a word.

"I see Preacher left me a leg," he smirked.

Raid nodded. "He's considerate like that."

Shadow smirked at the man as he picked up Cassie's now famous bat. He drew back his arm and hit the pricks left leg, with all the strength he had, just below the knee. Bull howled in pain, as the bones snapped, and one stuck out of his leg.

"Now you look like Tiffany," he said proudly. "Unfortunately, Preacher and me decided to keep you alive for a couple days, so there isn't a lot else I can do," he told the biker. "But being a former Navy Seal, I have something that I've had experience in."

There was a knock on the door, and Shadow answered, taking the bag from Dragon. He had made arrangements earlier, for the brother to pick him up a few things, and deliver them at a certain time. Dragon was right on time.

Shadow took the bag over to the bench, and the three brothers curiously peered inside. Shadow removed the only two objects in the bag, a jug of water and a towel.

"In the Seals, you train hard," he explained to a very pissed off Bull. "Water boarding is something all Seals have to learn to get through. We get it done to us early on, and we get to practice it on our teammates."

He moved over to Bull and stood right in front of him. Sniper moved behind the man, and grabbed his hair, yanking the man's head back roughly. Shadow then placed the towel directly over the man's face. Bull was screaming and thrashing, but the brothers ignored him. Shadow took the jug of water and removed the cap. Then he tipped the bottle and poured the water directly onto the man's face.

Bull instantly thrashed harder and choked. Shadow stopped pouring, and gave the biker a minute, to get his breath back. Sniper pushed the bikers head forward, and Shadow stepped back, as the man threw up the water.

The men repeated the process four more times. Finally, the biker had threw up all he could, and Shadow knew if he did it one more time, he'd kill him. He left the items on the bench, and turned, walking right back out the door. His turn was done, now he'd wait a couple days for the biker to heal, then they'd finish him together. The biker was now on borrowed time.

Chapter Forty Four
Tiffany

Tiffany couldn't be happier, to be leaving the hospital. It was two days later, and Doc had given her the okay to head back to the compound. She hadn't been bored during her stay. The bikers had all visited lots, and so had the girls. It had relieved Tiffany to see Cassie's arm wasn't as bad as she thought.

Shadow had also pretty much moved into the hospital while she was there. He had left for a few hours that first morning, then he had come back with a bag, and camped out. She had been over the moon about that, not wanting to admit that she didn't want to be alone.

Doc had pulled rank, and got her a slightly bigger bed, and she had fallen asleep each night in Shadow's arms. Navaho had also visited lots, promptly arriving at meal times to dump the hospital food the nurses delivered, and replace it with his own. The nurses had been furious with him, but then he'd smiled at them, and they'd ended up walking out in a daze.

Shadow carefully helped her dress, in a long skirt Ali had lent her. Apparently, she had gone through something similar with her leg, and said the long skirts were the easiest things to wear. After changing, Tiffany agreed completely. The skirt made it so that the stint fit easily underneath it. Ali promised that later that day, she'd take the girls to the mall, and they'd load up on skirts, so Tiffany would have her own.

Finally, Doc arrived with the wheelchair. Tiffany could only stare at it. It was the nicest wheelchair she had ever seen. If there was a Jaguar of wheelchairs, this was it.

"Where the fuck did you get that," Shadow asked in amazement.

"I borrowed it," Doc whispered quietly. "And don't ask where I borrowed it from," he ordered. "Tiffany will be in this for a while, so I wanted it to be a comfortable one."

Shadow shrugged his shoulders, then lifted Tiffany up, and gently placed her in it. She was happy to see it had a footrest that extended out, so she could keep her leg straight, like the stint forced it. Ten minutes later, they were out the door and headed to a black truck, that had her brother behind the wheel.

As soon as he saw them, Preacher jumped out, and opened the back door for them. Shadow then lifted her up and set her across the backseat. He got her seatbelt on, without hurting her chest, while Preacher folded up the wheelchair, and hefted it up into the back.

After both men got into the front, they were on their way home. Tiffany smiled at her brother, when she caught his eye in the mirror, and lounged back against the door. Ten minutes later they were passing through the gates.

She could only gape when she saw all the bikers were lined up in front of the clubhouse. When Shadow lifted her out, it was to a huge round of applause, and it made feel like she was part of the family. She beamed at them, and waved her thanks, as Shadow carried her to his room.

When he pushed open the door, he stopped dead, as he eyed the changes someone had made to his room. His quilt was now pink, and there was a pink rug on the floor, but it was the rest of the room that had him stunned. Flowers and plants were everywhere. They were sitting on the floor, they were covering his dresser, they were hanging from the ceiling, and it looked like shelving had been added to the walls, so they could be placed there as well. His room was now a living jungle.

"Oh my god," Tiffany cried. "It's amazing. I absolutely love it."

"Of course you would," Shadow grumbled. "Fucking bikers," he complained.

Roars of laughter sounded from the hall behind him, so Shadow took a couple steps in, and slammed the door.

Chapter Forty Five
Shadow

Shadow and Tiffany spent the first night in their jungle, with the windows open. Tiffany really liked it, but even she admitted to him, that some of the flowers were strong. Shadow knew once it was down to just the plants, it would be much better.

The brothers also surprised him, by starting his cabin. He was shocked, but thrilled, to see that they did the floor, the walls were up, and the roof was on. With no more threats at the moment, and nothing much going on, all the brothers had helped out with the build. They were pretty sure they would have the cabin done in just over a week.

This morning everyone was in the common room, and Navaho had prepared a huge breakfast. Tiffany sat in her wheelchair between Shadow and Preacher, and she looked happy. The poor girl had been tortured and broken, not once but twice, and she looked like she was completely at ease. She was laughing with the brothers as she ate.

As soon as they were done, Preacher motioned Shadow to the side of the room. Shadow gave her a quick kiss, then they moved away.

"I think it's time to end Bull. We haven't touched him in days, and I don't want him here, with Tiffany and the girls close. I know he's in no condition to do anything, but I don't want them breathing his fucking air," Preacher growled.

"Agreed," Shadow told him. "So we head over with a couple brothers and leave Tiffany here with the rest. She'll be okay for the next hour or two." The men turned to head back to Tiffany, but were surprised to see her glaring at them both.

"You're going to kill Bull now," she accused. Both men looked at her in concern.

"Now Tiff," Preacher tried to sooth. "You need to sit there and finish your breakfast. You will not be a part of this, you've been through enough already."

Shadow watched, as Tiffany picked up a piece of toast, from the pile left in the middle of the table, and threw it at Preacher. Shadow roared in laughter, as it hit the brother on his cheek, and stuck. Then he stopped, when a second piece of bread hit him, in exactly the same spot.

"Fuck Tiff," Preacher roared, as he peeled the bread off his face. "What the fuck did you do that for?"

"You want me to stay here, and you want me happy, then you let me be there when you kill him." She held up her hand when the men protested. "I don't want to help, I just want to see him take his last breath," she told them.

"He hurt me," she admitted sadly. "And I'm terrified of him. I just need to see him die, so I know I'll be completely free of him. I need this put behind me," she sighed.

Steele moved to her and started pushing her wheelchair towards the door. "You can stay with me sweetheart," he told her. "I'll let you sit in the corner. You'll be out of the way, but you'll be able to watch."

When Steele reached the door, he stopped, to turn and look back at the brothers. "You fuckers gonna come, or are you gonna break Tiffany's heart, but not granting her this," he growled.

Both the brothers dropped their heads, then followed Steele to the door. When Shadow reached Tiffany, he lifted her from the wheelchair, and carried her to the shed. Steele folded up the wheelchair and trailed behind them.

When they reached the shed, Steele went in first, and set up the wheelchair in the corner. Then Shadow gently set her down.

"You okay baby girl," he asked, as he crouched down in front of her. She looked at him, then she looked at Bull.

"I'm okay," she told him.

"That's my girl," he said, as he kissed her head. "Let's get this fucking done," he told the brothers.

Chapter Forty Six
Shadow

Shadow made sure Tiffany was comfortable in the corner before facing Steele.

"She shows any signs she's in pain, or looks like she can't handle this, you get her the hell out of here," he ordered Steele.

Steele didn't say a word, but he nodded in agreement. Before they could start, the door opened, and in walked Navaho, Dragon and Trike. They nodded in greeting, then moved to stand around Tiffany, showing their support, and being protective. Trike even went as far as to sit on the floor, right in front of her. He leaned back against the wheel, and crossed his arms, as he settled in.

"Thank you," she whispered quietly to all the brothers, then she turned back to face Bull. Shadow and Preacher took that to mean she was ready, so they turned back to Bull.

"How you doing today fucker," Preacher said, as he kicked at the bikers broken legs.

Bull lifted his head, and gritted his teeth, as his body rocked back and forth, from the swing of the chains. Shadow studied the man's legs for a minute, and noticed one had pus leaking from it, where the bone had come through. He moved towards the ass and poked at it with his boot. He chuckled, when Bull howled in pain.

"I think that hurts," Dagger said helpfully from the door. "Sorry I'm late, I had to wash my hair," he said seriously. "You can start now."

Steele snorted at the man. "Even at a time like this, you got a joke."

"I'm here all night," Dagger replied, as he winked at Steele.

"Fucking knock it off," Preacher ordered, as he picked up a large knife and handed it to Shadow. "I already added a decoration to the assholes chest, I image you want to add your own," he said.

Shadow nodded, as he grabbed the handle, and twirled it in his fist. He approached Bull slowly and dragged the knife back and forth across his chest. Several shallow cuts appeared, and the blood began to flow.

"You hurt my baby girl," he growled. "So I'm gonna hurt you." He increased the pressure, and the cuts began to go deeper. Bull twisted in the chains as he roared out in pain. Blood now dripped on the floor. Shadow took a minute to glance at Tiffany, and was pleased to see, that even though she was pale, she seemed to be okay.

Preacher then filled a shallow basin with water and dragged it to Bulls feet. Since the man was wearing nothing but pants, it was a simple task of lifting his bare feet, and placing them in the basin. Then he dragged the battery closer and fired it up. Bull was thrashing now and had turned a sickly green colour.

Preacher turned the dial to a low setting and touched the cables to Bulls bloody chest. Bull screamed, as sparks flew, and his body went ramrod straight. As soon as Preacher removed them, Bull's body slumped forward.

Dagger clapped from the corner and yelled again. Shadow chuckled once more as he took the cables from Preacher. He set the dial just a bit higher and took his turn. Again, sparks flew, and his body went straight. Shadow left them on a minute longer, then pulled them away. Bull was now sweating, and his skin was turning a bright red.

Preacher and Shadow then took turns, over the next hour, turning the dial a bit higher each round. Bull passed out several times, and they had to douse the man over the head with cold water. The water actually steamed when it hit the fuckers skin.

Both brothers looked at each other and decided Bull was done. The biker was barely conscious, and they had dragged his death out over four days. They were also very aware that Tiffany was watching. She had been watching for an hour, and she had smelt the burning skin.

Shadow drew his gun and passed it to Preacher. The prez took it and walked up to Bull. He lifted the man's head by his hair and glared at him.

"You fucker, have been sentenced to death." Then he put his gun right over Bull's heart and pulled the trigger. The brothers instantly became a human wall, standing directly in front of Tiffany, and blocking her view.

Finally, Shadow thought, this was over.

Chapter Forty Seven
Tiffany

Tiffany had a bit of an upset stomach after watching Bull's death. She had been relieved when all the bikers had blocked her view. She knew the man was dead, and she really didn't need to see all the blood. As soon as it was over, Shadow was motioning for the brothers to get her out of there.

"I have to shower before I touch you baby girl," he told her. "The brothers will keep you company in the common room. I'll head in through the back door, then come to you when I'm done."

She nodded, and then wrapped her arms around Trike's neck, as he carefully picked her up. Again Steele folded up her wheelchair and carried it onto the main building. By the time Trike had carried her inside, he had the wheelchair set back up for her. She was happy to see the girls waiting for her.

An hour later, she was a lot more relaxed, and her stomach had settled. The girls had kept her entertained, with stories about how the bikers had decorated their rooms. She was surprised to find out it seemed to be a tradition when a biker found his One. When she asked who was responsible, none of the girls answered. They all speculated that it was most likely Dagger, but they didn't know for sure.

She smiled happily at Shadow when he finally joined them. He looked clean, and for once he looked completely relaxed. In the entire time she had known him, she'd never seen him like this. He looked good carefree. He smirked when he caught her watching him.

"You see something you like," he asked her.

"I do," she told him happily.

"Don't you dare start that shit in front of me," Preacher roared, from a stool at the bar. He had finished his shower before Shadow and had joined them a few minutes earlier. "That's my baby sister," he complained.

"Maybe we should spend some time in our room," Shadow said, as he smiled down at her.

Trike immediately jumped to his feet. "Wait, before you run away, there's something I want to tell everyone," he said. Practically the entire club was converged in the common room. After Bull's death, they all wanted to be there together.

Tiffany watched, as Misty suddenly stood, and went to stand beside him. As soon as she got close, Trike grabbed her around the waist, and pulled her into his side.

"Misty was hurt pretty bad, after the things Carly and the prospects did to her," Trike explained. "We weren't sure how well she would heal. After we got married, she shared some news with me, but Doc advised us to wait awhile before sharing it with all of you. He just wanted to make sure everything was okay first," he said.

"I'm pregnant," Misty said happily. "And I just passed my first trimester."

All at once, the entire room erupted in applause. Bikers rose from their chairs and headed for the couple. Trike got pats on the back, and man hugs, while Misty got kisses on the cheek, and biker hugs. Trike tolerated it for a while, then he blew.

"That's enough fucking kissing and hugging," he roared. "You can congratulate her from across the room." The men all laughed, as they ignored Trike, and kept on kissing and hugging Misty.

Shadow chose that moment to surprise Tiffany and lifted her out of her chair.

"I think it's time for some celebrating of our own baby girl," he told her. She smiled up at him, and kissed his cheek, agreeing with him in her own way. As soon as they were back in the room, and she was lying on the bed, she lost her smile.

"Make love to me," she ordered. "I want this day to end on a perfect note. Everything's over now, and I want my time with you to begin."

Shadow smiled down at her, and she knew he wouldn't say no. So, for the rest of the night, he made slow, torturous love to her. He was gentle and caring, and not once did she experience any pain. It was a night she would never forget.

Epilogue

Two weeks later, the cabin was officially done. It took a little longer, but Shadow wanted everything just right. It was beautiful inside, and he hoped Tiffany liked it.

When he finally showed it to her, she sat on the chesterfield and cried. At first it worried him that she hated it, but when he knelt in front of her and he lifted her tear stained face, the smiled he was greeted with took his breath away. She slid to the floor, and sat on his lap, giving him a kiss that turned heated.

He had painted the inside of the cabin, a beautiful pale green. He had added touches of creams and beiges, with a splash of a stunning rust colour. Then he had filled the cabin with every single plant that the brothers had filled his room with. Since the space was bigger than his room, the plants fit better, and it wasn't quite so overwhelming. Even he was surprised at how nice it turned out.

"Marry me," he told her. "Say yes, and we'll take time to get to know each other, without all the drama surrounding us. Say yes, and I'll make you the happiest girl ever. Say yes, and I'll never let you be hurt again. Say yes, and I'll love you for the rest of your life," he said, as he stroked her cheek.

"Yes," she whispered back. "But I say yes, to making you just as happy. I say yes, to protecting you, just as much as you protect me. And I say yes, to loving you for the rest of my life," she told him, as she covered his hand, that still rested on her cheek.

With her free hand, she balled it into a tight fist, and placed it over her heart, just as he did when her brother had separated them. Laughing, he immediately returned the gesture, and her heart swelled.

"The first time I saw you lying in that room, broken and battered at Bull's compound, I knew I would do whatever it took to save you. When you locked eyes with me, I knew you were going to change my life," he told her.

Then he took a ring out of his pocket and slipped it on her finger. When she looked down, she was surprised to see how beautiful it was. There was a stunning diamond in the middle, and tiny gold flowers surrounded it. She knew it was a ring she'd proudly wear forever.

"I love it," she told him. "My legs slowly getting better. Give me three months, I'll work hard, and I'll follow all Doc's orders, then I'll be able to walk down the isle to you. Doc said I'll probably have a limp, but I won't be in my chair."

"Perfect," he said. "Then we'll set the day for three months from today." Then he reached behind the couch and pulled out a box. She watched as he took out a leather vest. She smiled as he held it out, so she could get a good look at it. She laughed, when she read the name Tiff on the name patch.

"Why Tiff," she asked curiously.

"Because baby girl's only for me," he told her affectionately. She lost the smile, when he turned it around, and she read property of Shadow on the back.

"It's perfect," she whispered.

They made love into the night, and exactly three months later, they were married by her brother. She worked hard, and even though she had to wear a brace, she was able to walk down the isle.

Surprisingly, Old Joe had followed through, and shown up for an extended visit. Tiffany was beyond words when she found out he had been the one to tell Shadow and Preacher where Bull had her. They had become close, and he had been the man to walk her down the isle.

It was finally time for the couple to be happy, and for the first time in both their lives, they had found themselves in a place they could call home.

About the Author

MEGAN FALL is a mother of three who helps her husband run his construction business. She has been writing all her life, but with a push from her daughter, started publishing. It's the best thing she ever did. When she's not writing, you can find her at the beach. She loves searching for rocks, sea glass, driftwood and fossils. She believes in ghosts, collects ridiculous amounts of plants, and rides on the back of her hubby's motorcycle.

MEGAN FALL

Look for these books coming soon!

STONE KNIGHTS MC SERIES
Finding Ali
Saving Cassie
Loving Misty
Rescuing Tiffany
Guarding Alexandria
Protecting Fable
Surviving November
Sheltering Macy
Defending Zoe

DEVILS SOLDIERS MC SERIES
Resisting Diesel
Surviving Hawk

THE ENFORCER SERIES
The Enforcer
The Enforcers Revenge

Guarding Alexandria
Stone Knight's Book 5

Chapter One
Alexandria

Alex stared out of the curtains, at the side of the stage. She was utterly and truly terrified. This was the worst idea she had ever come up with. How she was supposed to do this, she had no idea. She tried to get her feet to move forward, but they wouldn't cooperate. The music was winding down now, and that meant it was almost her turn.

She looked down at her ridiculous outfit. She had outrageously high red heels on, a plaid miniskirt that barely covered her, and a white blouse that only had one button done up, and was tied just under her breasts. Her hair was up in a ponytail, and it was held with a long plaid ribbon.

This was the first night of her new stripping career. The girls had been training her for a week now, and they promised she was ready. Luckily, her boss let the new girls strip down to their underwear for their first week, so she wouldn't be totally naked up there. At least, not for a bit yet. The red bra and panty set were skimpy, but they covered all her essential parts.

Finally, the music from the last stripper stopped. She smiled, as Candy sauntered past with an arm full of clothes. Candy winked at her, and gave her a huge smile, then headed for the dressing room. She heard the MC announce her and cringed at her new stripper name.

"And tonight we have a newbie for your enjoyment. She's a little shy, she's a little unsure, but she's exceptionally stunning. Please welcome to the stage, for the first time ever, Sweet Pea."

The crowd of men roared as Alex sauntered on stage. She swayed her hips to the Three Days Grace song Pain as she moved towards the stage. She blocked out the men around her as she concentrated on the song. When she reached the pole, she grabbed on and closed her eyes.

Dancing was second nature to her, she did it all the time, but it was always in private. Her father had built her a small studio in the basement, and she spent hours every day down there. She had no formal training, but the other strippers had been in awe of her. She even got to show them a few moves.

Alex moved with the music, completely comfortable on the pole. She slid up and down, then flipped over, so her pony dragged on the ground. With her eyes still closed, she slid to the floor, then removed her top. Grabbing the pole again, she rubbed against it, and removed her hair ribbon. Her long blonde hair flew around her as she twirled around the pole.

She kicked off her heels, then grabbed the pole and flipped over again. With her bare feet she had better traction, so she moved up the pole, while still upside down. Then she flipped again and removed her skirt. Now only in her underwear, she climbed high and held on with one hand. Then she threw out her free arm, and spun all the way back to the ground, as her song ended.

They threw whistles, catcalls and crude comments her way, but she ignored them. Keeping her eyes down, she grabbed her clothes and hurried from the stage. There was a girl that came out in between the acts, and collected the money, so she didn't have to worry about that.

She hurried to the change room and threw on her yoga pants and t-shirt. They only expected her to do one dance on her first night.

Tomorrow it would be two, and the night after that three. Three was the norm most girls did in a night unless they were short staffed.

Her boss was also pushing her to walk the floor in between dances. Apparently, most of the girls did lap dances, and that's where the money was. Alex didn't think she could ever do that though. Her boss was understanding, and said it was up to her, but he warned her he'd keep asking.

The girl that collected her money came in, and handed her a stack of bills, then turned without a word and left again. Alex grabbed her things and headed for the door. Drew was there waiting for her, he was the huge bouncer that walked most of the girls to their cars. She took his arm, and smiled up at him, as he showed her out.

Her first night was over, and she had survived, but a tear rolled down her cheek. Things were bad right now, but she knew tonight she had just made them worse. She had sunk low, and now there was no turning back.

Made in the USA
Middletown, DE
08 September 2018